THE SHERIFF'S SON

Center Point
Large Print

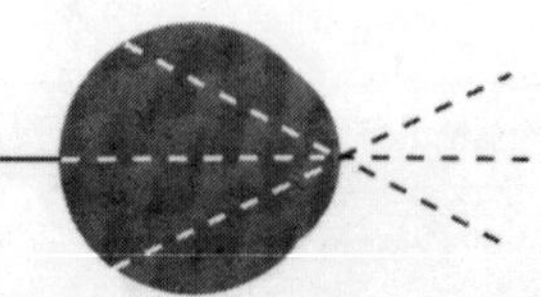

This Large Print Book carries the
Seal of Approval of N.A.V.H.

THE SHERIFF'S SON

WILLIAM MACLEOD RAINE

CENTER POINT PUBLISHING
THORNDIKE, MAINE

This Center Point Large Print edition
is published in the year 2004 by arrangement with
Golden West Literary Agency.

The text of this Large Print edition is unabridged. In other aspects, this book may vary from the original edition. Printed in Thailand. Set in 16-point Times New Roman type by Bill Coskrey and Gary Socquet.

ISBN 1-58547-423-1

Library of Congress Cataloging-in-Publication Data

Raine, William MacLeod, 1871-1954.
The sheriff's son / William MacLeod Raines.--Center Point large print ed.
p. cm.
ISBN 1-58547-423-1 (lib. bdg. : alk. paper)
1. Large type books. I. Title.

PS3535.A385S54 2004
813'.2--dc22

2003023668

To

ROBERT H. DAVIS

Who with His Usual Generosity to
Writers Made the Author a Present
of the Germ Idea of this Plot

CONTENTS

FOREWORD

Through the mesquite a horse moved deviously, following the crooked trail of least resistance. A man was in the saddle and in front of him a little boy nodding with sleep. The arm of the rider cradled the youngster against the lurches of the pony's gait.

The owner of the arm looked down at the tired little bundle it was supporting. A wistful tenderness was in the leathery face. To the rest of the world he was a man of iron. To this wee bit of humanity he was a nurse, a playmate, a slave.

"We're 'most to the creek now, son. Onc't we get there, we'll throw off and camp. You can eat a snack and tumble right off to bye-low land," he promised.

The five-year-old smiled faintly and snuggled closer. His long lashes drooped again to the soft cheeks. With the innocent selfishness of a child he accepted the love that sheltered him from all troubles.

A valley opened below the mesa, the trail falling abruptly almost from the hoofs of the horse. Beaudry drew up and looked down. From rim to rim the meadow was perhaps half a mile across. Seen from above, the bed of it was like an emerald lake through which wound a ribbon of silver. This ribbon was Big Creek. To the right it emerged from a draw in the foothills where green reaches of forest rose tier after tier toward the purple mountains. Far up among these peaks Big Creek had its source in Lost Lake, which lay at the foot of a glacier near the top of the world.

The saw-toothed range lifted its crest into a sky of

violet haze. Half an hour since the sun had set in a blaze of splendor behind a crotch of the hills, but dusk had softened the vivid tints of orange and crimson and scarlet to a faint pink glow. Already the mountain silhouette had lost its sharp edge and the outlines were blurring. Soon night would sift down over the roof of the continent.

The eyes of the man searched warily the valley below. They rested closely on the willows by the ford, the cottonwood grove to the left, and the big rocks beyond the creek. From its case beneath his leg he took the sawed-off shotgun loaded with buckshot. It rested on the pommel of the saddle while his long and careful scrutiny swept the panorama. The spot was an ideal one for an ambush.

His unease communicated itself to the boy, who began to whimper softly. Beaudry, distressed, tried to comfort him.

"Now, don't you, son—don't you. Dad ain't going to let anything hurt you-all."

Presently he touched the flank of his roan with a spur and the animal began to pick its way down the steep trail among the loose rubble. Not for an instant did the rider relax his vigilance as he descended. At the ford he examined the ground carefully to make sure that nobody had crossed since the shower of the afternoon. Swinging to the saddle again, he put his horse to the water and splashed through to the opposite shore. Once more he dismounted and studied the approach to the creek. No tracks had written their story on the sand in the past few hours. Yet with every sense alert he led the way to the cottonwood grove where he intended to camp. Not till he had made a tour of the big rocks and a clump of prickly pears adjoining was his mind easy.

He came back to find the boy crying. "What's the matter, big son?" he called cheerily. "Nothing a-tall to be afraid of. This nice camping-ground fits us like a coat of paint. You-all take forty winks while dad fixes up some supper."

He spread his slicker and rolled his coat for a pillow, fitting it snugly to the child's head. While he lit a fire he beguiled the time with animated talk. One might have guessed that he was trying to make the little fellow forget the alarm that had been stirred in his mind.

"Sing the li'l' ole hawss," commanded the boy, reducing his sobs.

Beaudry followed orders in a tuneless voice that hopped gayly up and down. He had invented words and music years ago as a lullaby and the song was in frequent demand.

> "Li'l' ole hawss an' li'l' ole cow,
> Amblin' along by the ole haymow,
> Li'l' ole hawss took a bite an' a chew,
> 'Durned if I don't,' says the ole cow, too."

Seventeen stanzas detailed the adventures of this amazing horse and predatory cow. Somewhere near the middle of the epic little Royal Beaudry usually dropped asleep. The rhythmic tale always comforted him. These nameless animals were very real friends of his. They had been companions of his tenderest years. He loved them with a devotion from which no fairy tale could wean him.

Before he had quite surrendered to the lullaby, his father aroused him to share the bacon and the flapjacks he had cooked.

"Come and get it, big son," Beaudry called with an imitation of manly roughness.

The boy ate drowsily before the fire, nodding between bites.

Presently the father wrapped the lad up snugly in his blankets and prompted him while he said his prayers. No woman's hands could have been tenderer than the calloused ones of this frontiersman. The boy was his life. For the girl-bride of John Beaudry had died to give his son birth.

Beaudry sat by the dying fire and smoked. The hills had faded to black, shadowy outlines beneath a night of a million stars. During the day the mountains were companions, heaven was the home of warm friendly sunshine that poured down lance-straight upon the traveler. But now the black, jagged peaks were guards that shut him into a vast prison of loneliness. He was alone with God, an atom of no consequence. Many a time, when he had looked up into the sky vault from the saddle that was his pillow, he had known that sense of insignificance.

To-night the thoughts of John Beaudry were somber. He looked over his past with a strange feeling that he had lived his life and come to the end of it. He was not yet forty, a well-set, bowlegged man of medium height, in perfect health, sound as to every organ. From an old war wound he had got while raiding with Morgan he limped a little. Two more recent bullet scars marked his body.

But none of these interfered with his activity. He was in the virile prime of life; yet a bell rang in his heart the warning that he was soon to die. That was why he was taking his little son out of the country to safety.

He took all the precautions that one could, but he knew that in the end these would fail him. The Rutherfords would get him. Of that he had no doubt. They would probably have killed him, anyhow, but he had made his sentence sure when he had shot Anse Rutherford and wounded Eli Schaick ten days ago. That it had been done by him in self-defense made no difference.

Out of the Civil War John Beaudry had come looking only for peace. He had moved West and been flung into the wild, turbulent life of the frontier. In the Big Creek country there was no peace for strong men in the seventies. It was a time and place for rustlers and horse-thieves to flourish at the expense of honest settlers. They elected their friends to office and laughed at the law.

But the tide of civilization laps forward. A cattlemen's association had been formed. Beaudry, active as an organizer, had been chosen its first president. With all his energy he had fought the rustlers. When the time came to make a stand the association nominated Beaudry for sheriff and elected him. He had prosecuted the thieves remorselessly in spite of threats and shots in the dark. Two of them had been put by him behind bars. Others were awaiting trial. The climax had come when he met Anse Rutherford and his companion at Battle Butte, had defeated them both singlehanded, and had left one dead on the field and the other badly wounded.

Men said that John Beaudry was one of the great sheriffs of the West. Perhaps he was, but he would have to pay the price that such a reputation exacts. The Rutherford gang had sworn his death and he knew they would keep the oath.

The man sat with one hand resting on the slim body of the sleeping boy. His heart was troubled. What was to become of little Royal without either father or mother? After the manner of men who live much alone in the open he spoke his thoughts aloud.

"Son, one of these here days they're sure a-goin' to get yore dad. Maybe he'll ride out of town and after a while the hawss will come galloping back with an empty saddle. A man can be mighty unpopular and die of old age, but not if he keeps bustin' up the plans of rampageous two-gun men, not if he shoots them up when they're full of the devil and bad whiskey. It ain't on the cyards for me to beat them to the draw every time, let alone that they'll see to it all the breaks are with them. No, sir. I reckon one of these days you're goin' to be an orphan, little son."

He stooped over the child and wrapped the blankets closer. The muscles of his tanned face twitched. Long he held the warm, slender body of the boy as close to him as he dared for fear of wakening him.

The man lay tense and rigid, his set face staring up into the starry night. It was his hour of trial. A rising tide was sweeping him away. He had to clutch at every straw to hold his footing. But something in the man—his lifetime habit of facing the duty that he saw—held him steady.

"You got to stand the gaff, Jack Beaudry. Can't run away from your job, can you? Got to go through, haven't you? Well, then!"

Peace came at last to the tormented man. He fell asleep. Hours later he opened his eyes upon a world bathed in light. It was such a brave warm world that the fears which had gripped him in the chill night seemed sinister dreams. In this clear, limpid atmosphere only a sick soul could believe in a blind alley from which there was no escape.

But facts are facts. He might hope for escape, but even now he could not delude himself with the thought that he might win through without a fight.

While they ate breakfast he told the boy about the mother whom he had never seen. John Beaudry had always intended to tell Royal the story of his love for the slender, sweet-lipped girl whose grace and beauty had flooded his soul. But the reticence of shyness had sealed his lips. He had cared for her with a reverence too deep for words.

She was the daughter of well-to-do people visiting in the West. The young cattleman and she had fallen in love almost at sight and had remained lovers till the day of her death. After one year of happiness tragedy had stalked their lives. Beaudry, even then the object of the rustlers' rage, had been intercepted on the way from Battle Butte to his ranch. His wife, riding to meet him, heard shots and galloped forward. From the mesa she looked down into a draw and saw her husband fighting for his life. He was at bay in a bed of boulders, so well covered by the big rocks that the rustlers could not easily get at him. His enemies, scattered fanshape across the entrance to the arroyo, were gradually edging nearer. In a panic of fear she rode wildly to the nearest ranch, gasped out her appeal for help, and collapsed in a woeful little huddle. His friends arrived in time to save Beaudry, damaged only to the extent of a flesh wound in the shoulder, but the next week the young wife gave premature birth to her child and died four days later.

In mental and physical equipment the baby was heir to the fears which had beset the last days of the mother. He was a frail little fellow and he whimpered at trifles. But the clutch of the tiny pink fingers held John Beaudry more firmly than a grip of steel. With unflagging patience he fended bogies from the youngster.

But the day was at hand when he could do this no longer. That was why he was telling Royal about the mother he had never known. From his neck he drew a light gold chain, at the end of which was a small square folding case. In it was a daguerreotype of a golden-haired, smiling girl who looked out at her son with an effect of shy eagerness.

"Give Roy pretty lady," demanded the boy.

Beaudry shook his head slowly. "I reckon that's 'most the only thing you can ask your dad for that he won't give you." He continued unsteadily, looking at the picture in the palm of his hand. "Lady-Bird I called her, son. She used to fill the house with music right out of her heart. . . . Fine as silk and true as gold. Don't you ever forget that your mother was a thoroughbred." His voice broke. "But I hadn't ought to have let her stay out here. She belonged where folks are good and kind, where they love books and music. Yet she wouldn't leave me because . . . because . . . Maybe you'll know why she wouldn't some day, little son."

He drew a long, ragged breath and slipped the case back under his shirt.

Quickly Beaudry rose and began to bustle about with suspicious cheerfulness. He whistled while he packed and saddled. In the fresh cool morning air they rode across the valley and climbed to the mesa beyond. The sun mounted higher and the heat shimmered on the trail in front of them. The surface of the earth was cracked in dry, sun-baked tiles curving upward at the edges. Cat's-claw clutched at the legs of the travelers. Occasionally a swift darted from rock to rock. The faint, low voices of the desert were inaudible when the horse moved. The riders came out of the silence and moved into the silence.

It was noon when Beaudry drew into the suburbs of Battle Butte. He took an inconspicuous way by alleys and side streets to the corral. His enemies might or might not be in town. He wanted to take no chances. All he asked was to postpone the crisis until Royal was safe aboard a train. Crossing San Miguel Street, the riders came face to face with a man Beaudry knew to be a spy of the Rutherfords. He was a sleek, sly little man named Chet Fox.

"Evenin', sheriff. Looks some like we-all might have rain," Fox said, rasping his unshaven chin with the palm of a hand.

"Looks like," agreed Beaudry with a curt nod and rode on.

Fox disappeared around a corner, hurried forward for half a block, and turned in at the Silver Dollar Saloon. A broad-shouldered, hawk-nosed man of thirty was talking to three of his friends. Toward this group Fox hurried. In a low voice he spoke six words that condemned John Beaudry to death.

"Beaudry just now rode into town."

Hal Rutherford forgot the story he was telling. He gave crisp, short orders. The men about him left by the back door of the saloon and scattered.

Meanwhile the sheriff rode into the Elephant Corral and unsaddled his horse. He led the animal to the trough in the yard and pumped water for it. His son trotted back beside him to the stable and played with a puppy while the roan was being fed.

Jake Sharp, owner of the corral, stood in the doorway and chatted with the sheriff for a minute. Was it true that a new schoolhouse was going to be built on Bonito? And had the sheriff heard whether McCarty was to be boss of Big Creek roundup?

Beaudry answered his questions and turned away. Royal clung to one hand as they walked. The other held the muley gun.

It was no sound that warned the sheriff. The approach of his enemies had been noiseless. But the sixth sense that comes to some fighting men made him look up quickly. Five riders were moving down the street toward the stable, Hal Rutherford in the lead. The alert glance of the imperiled man swept the pasture back of the corral. The glint of the sun heliographed danger from the rifle barrels of two men just topping the brow of the hill. Two more were stealing up through a draw to the right. A bullet whistled past the head of the officer.

The father spoke quietly to his little boy. "Run, son, to the stable."

The little chap began to sob. Bullets were already kicking up the dust behind them. Roy clung in terror to the leg of his father.

Beaudry caught up the child and made a dash for the stable. He reached it, just as Sharp and his horse-wrangler were disappearing into the loft. There was no time to climb the ladder with Royal. John flung open the top of the feed-bin, dropped the boy inside, and slammed down the lid.

The story of the fight that followed is still an epic in the Southwest. There was no question of fair play. The enemies of the sheriff intended to murder him.

The men in his rear were already clambering over the corral fence. One of them had a scarlet handkerchief around his neck. Beaudry fired from his hip and the vivid kerchief lurched forward into the dust. Almost at the same moment a sharp sting in the fleshy part of his leg told the officer that he was wounded.

From front and rear the attackers surged into the stable. The sheriff emptied the second barrel of buckshot into the huddle and retreated into an empty horse-stall. The smoke of many guns filled the air so that the heads thrust at him seemed oddly detached from bodies. A red-hot flame burned its way through his chest. He knew he was mortally wounded.

Hal Rutherford plunged at him, screaming an oath. "We've got him, boys."

Beaudry stumbled back against the manger, the arms of his foe clinging to him like ropes of steel. Twice he brought down the butt of his sawed-off gun on the black head of Rutherford. The grip of the big hillman grew lax, and as the man collapsed, his fingers slid slackly down the thighs of the officer.

John dropped the empty weapon and dragged out a Colt's forty-four. He fired low and fast, not stopping to take aim. Another flame seared its way through his body. The time left him now could be counted in seconds.

But it was not in the man to give up. The old rebel yell of Morgan's raiders quavered from his throat. They rushed him.

With no room even for six-gun work he turned his revolver into a club. His arm rose and fell in the mêlée as the drive of the rustlers swept him to and fro.

So savage was the defense of their victim against the hillmen's onslaught that he beat them off. A sudden panic seized them, and those that could still travel fled in terror.

They left behind them four dead and two badly wounded. One would be a cripple to the day of his death. Of those who escaped there was not one that did not carry scars for months as a memento of the battle.

The sheriff was lying in the stall when Sharp found him. From out of the feed-bin the owner of the corral brought his boy to the father whose life was ebbing. The child was trembling like an aspen leaf.

"Picture," gasped Beaudry, his hand moving feebly toward the chain.

A bullet had struck the edge of the daguerreotype case.

"She . . . tried . . . to save me . . . again," murmured the dying man with a faint smile.

He looked at the face of his sweetheart. It smiled an eager invitation to him. A strange radiance lit his eyes.

Then his head fell back. He had gone to join his Lady-Bird.

CHAPTER 1

DINGWELL GIVES THREE CHEERS

Dave Dingwell had been in the saddle almost since daylight had wakened him to the magic sunshine of a world washed cool and miraculously clean by the soft breath of the hills. Steadily he had jogged across the desert toward the range. Afternoon had brought him to the foothills, where a fine rain blotted out the peaks and softened the sharp outlines of the landscape to a gentle blur of green loveliness.

The rider untied his slicker from the rear of the saddle and slipped into it. He had lived too long in sun-and-wind-parched New Mexico to resent a shower. Yet he realized that it might seriously affect the success of what he had undertaken.

If there had been any one to observe this solitary traveler, he would have said that the man gave no heed to the beauty of the day. Since he had broken camp his impassive gaze had been fixed for the most part on the ground in front of him. Occasionally he swung his long leg across the rump of the horse and dismounted to stoop down for a closer examination of the hoofprints he was following. They were not recent tracks. He happened to know that they were about three days old. Plain as a printed book was the story they told him.

The horses that had made these tracks had been ridden by men in a desperate hurry. They had walked little and galloped much. Not once had they fallen into the easy Spanish jog-trot used so much in the casual travel of the

Southwest. The spur of some compelling motive had driven this party at top speed.

Since Dingwell knew the reason for such haste he rode warily. His alert caution suggested the panther. The eye of the man pounced surely upon every bit of cactus or greasewood behind which a possible foe might be hidden. His lean, sun-tanned face was an open letter of recommendation as to his ability to take care of himself in a world that had often glared at him wolfishly. A man in a temper to pick a quarrel would have looked twice at Dave Dingwell before choosing him as the object of it—and then would have passed on to a less competent citizen.

The trail grew stiffer. It circled into a draw down which tumbled a jocund little stream. Trout, it might be safely guessed, lurked here in the riffles and behind the big stones. An ideal camping-ground this, but the rider rejected it apparently without consideration. He passed into the cañon beyond, and so by a long uphill climb came to the higher reaches of the hills.

He rode patiently, without any hurry, without any hesitation. Here again a reader of character might have found something significant in the steadiness of the man. Once on the trail, it would not be easy to shake him off.

By the count of years Dingwell might be in the early forties. Many little wrinkles radiated fanlike from the corners of his eyes. But whatever his age time had not tamed him. In the cock of those same steel-blue eyes was something jaunty, something almost debonair, that carried one back to a youth of care-free rioting in a land of sunshine. Not that Mr. Dingwell was given to futile dissipations. He had the reputation of a responsible ranchman. But it is not to be denied that little devils of mischief at times danced in those orbs.

Into the hills the trail wound across gulches and along the shoulders of elephant humps. It brought him into a country of stunted pines and red sandstone, and so to the summit of a ridge which formed part of the rim of a saucer-shaped basin. He looked down into an open park hedged in on the far side by mountains. Scrubby pines straggled up the slopes from arroyos that cleft the hills. By divers unknown paths these led into the range beyond.

A clump of quaking aspens was the chief landmark in the bed of the park. Though this was the immediate destination of Mr. Dingwell, since the hoofprints he was following plunged straight down toward the grove, yet he took certain precautions before venturing nearer. He made sure that the 45-70 Winchester that lay across the saddle was in working order. Also he kept along the rim of the saucer-shaped park till he came to a break where a creek tumbled down in a white foam through a ravine.

"It's a heap better to be safe than to be sorry," he explained to himself cheerfully. "They call this Lonesome Park, and maybe so it deserves its name to-day. But you never can tell, Dave. We'll make haste slowly if you don't mind."

Along the bank of the creek he descended, letting his sure-footed cowpony pick its own way while he gave strict attention to the scenery. At a bend of the stream he struck again the trail of the riders he had been following and came from there directly to the edge of the aspen clump.

Apparently his precautions were unnecessary. He was alone. There could be no doubt of that. Only the tracks of feet and the ashes of a dead fire showed that within a few days a party had camped here.

Dingwell threw his bridle to the ground and with his rifle tucked under his arm examined the tracks carefully. Sometimes he was down on hands and knees peering at the faint marks of which he was reading the story. Foot by foot he quartered over the sand, entirely circling the grove before he returned to the ashes of the dead fire. Certain facts he had discovered. One was that the party which had camped here had split up and taken to the hills by different trails instead of as a unit. Still another was that so far as he could see there had been no digging in or near the grove.

It was raining more definitely now, so that the distant peaks were hidden in a mist. In the lee of the aspens it was still dry. Dingwell stood there frowning at the ashes of the dead camp-fire. He had had a theory, and it was not working out quite as he had hoped. For the moment he was at a mental impasse. Part of what had happened he could guess almost as well as if he had been present to see it. Sweeney's posse had given the fugitives a scare at Dry Gap and driven them back into the desert. In the early morning they had tried the hills again and had reached Lonesome Park. But they could not be sure that Sweeney or some one of the posses sent out by the railroad was not close at hand. Somewhere in the range back of them the pursuers were combing the hills, and into those very hills the bandits had to go to disappear in their mountain haunts.

Even before reaching the park Dingwell had guessed the robbers would separate here and strike each for individual safety. But what had they done with the loot? That was the thing that puzzled him.

They had divided the gold here. Or one of them had taken it with him to an appointed rendezvous in the hills. Or they had cached it. One of these three plans had been followed. But which?

Dingwell rubbed the open fingers of one hand slowly through his sunburnt thatch of hair. "Doggone my hide, if it don't look like they took it with them," he murmured. "But that ain't reasonable, Dave. The man in charge of this hold-up knew his business. It was smooth work all the way through. If it hadn't been for bad luck he would have got away with the whole thing fine. They still had the loot with them when they got here. No doubt about that. Well, then! He wouldn't divvy up here, because, if they separated, and any one of them got caught with the gold on him, it would be a give-away. But if they didn't have the dough on them, it would not matter if some of the boys were caught. You can't do anything with a man riding peaceable through the hills looking for strays, no matter how loaded to the guards with suspicions you may be. So they would cache the loot. Wouldn't they? Sure they would if they had any sense. But tell me where, Dave."

His thoughtful eyes had for some moments been resting on something that held them. He stooped and picked up a little chip of sealing-wax. Instantly he knew how it had come here. The gold sacks had been sealed by the express company with wax. At least one of the sacks had been opened here by the robbers.

Did this mean they had divided their treasure here? It might mean that. Or it might mean that before they cached it they had opened one sack to see how much it held. Dingwell clung to the opinion that the latter was the truth, partly because this marched with his hopes and partly because it seemed to him more likely. There would be a big risk in taking their haul with them farther. There was none at all in caching it.

It was odd how that little heap of ashes in the center of the camp-fire drew his eye. Ashes did not arrange themselves that way naturally. Some one had raked these into a pile. Why? And who?

He could not answer those questions offhand. But he had a large bump of curiosity about some things. Otherwise he would not have been where he was that afternoon. With his boot he swept the ashes aside. The ground beneath them was a little higher than it was in the immediate neighborhood. Why should the bandits have built their fire on a small hillock when there was level ground adjacent? There might be a reason underneath that little rise of ground or there might not. Mr. Dingwell got out his long hunting-knife, fell on his knees, and began to dig at the center of the spot where the camp-fire had been.

The dirt flew. With his left hand he scooped it from the hole he was making. Presently the point of his knife struck metal. Three minutes later he unearthed a heavy gunnysack. Inside of it were a lot of smaller sacks bearing the seal of the Western Express Company. He had found the gold stolen by the Rutherford gang from the Pacific Flyer.

Dave was pleased with himself. It had been a good day's work. He admitted cheerfully that there was not another man in New Mexico who could have pulled off successfully the thing he had just done. The loot had been well hidden. It had been a stroke of genius to cache it in the spot where the camp-fire was afterward built. But he had outguessed Jess Tighe that time. His luck had sure stood up fine. The occasion called for a demonstration.

He took off his broad-rimmed gray hat. "Three rousing cheers, Mr. Dingwell," he announced ceremoniously. "Now, all together."

Rising to his toes, he waved his hat joyously, worked his shoulders like a college cheer leader, and gave a dumb pantomime of yelling. He had intended to finish off with a short solo dance step, for it is not every day that a man finds twenty thousand dollars in gold bars buried in the sand.

But he changed his mind. As he let himself slowly down to his heels there was a sardonic grin on his brown face. In outguessing Tighe he had slipped one little mental cog, after all, and the chances were that he would pay high for his error. A man had been lying in the mesquite close to the creek watching him all the time. He knew it because he had caught the flash of light on the rifle barrel that covered him.

The gold-digger beckoned with his hat as he called out. "Come right along to the party. You're welcome as a frost in June."

A head raised itself cautiously out of the brush. "Don't you move, or I'll plug lead into you."

"I'm hog-tied," answered Dingwell promptly.

His mind worked swiftly. The man with the drop on him was Chet Fox, a hanger-on of the Rutherford gang, just as he had been seventeen years before when he betrayed John Beaudry to death. Fox was shrewd and wily, but no gunman. If Chet was alone, his prisoner did not propose to remain one. Dave did not intend to make any fool breaks, but it would be hard luck if he could not contrive a chance to turn the tables.

"Reach for the roof."

Dingwell obeyed orders.

Fox came forward very cautiously. Not for an instant did his beady eyes lift from the man he covered.

"Turn your back to me."

The other man did as he was told.

Gingerly Fox transferred the rifle to his left hand, then drew a revolver. He placed the rifle against the fork of a young aspen and the barrel of the six-gun against the small of Dingwell's back.

"Make just one break and you're a goner," he threatened.

With deft fingers he slid the revolver of the cattleman from its holster. Then, having collected Dingwell's rifle, he fell back a few steps.

"Now you can go on with those health exercises I interrupted if you've a mind to," Fox suggested with a sneer.

His prisoner turned dejected eyes upon him. "That's right. Rub it in, Chet. Don't you reckon I know what a long-eared jackass I am?"

"There's two of us know it then," said Fox dryly. "Now, lift that gunnysack to your saddle and tie it on behind."

This done, Fox pulled himself to the saddle, still with a wary eye on his captive.

"Hit the trail along the creek," he ordered.

Dingwell moved forward reluctantly. It was easy to read chagrin and depression in the sag of his shoulders and the drag of his feet.

The pig eyes of the fat little man on horseback shone with triumph. He was enjoying himself hugely. It was worth something to have tamed so debonair a dare-devil as Dingwell had the reputation of being. He had the fellow so meek that he would eat out of his hand.

CHAPTER 2

DAVE CACHES A GUNNYSACK

Fox rode about ten yards behind his prisoner, who plodded without spirit up the creek trail that led from the basin.

"You're certainly an accommodating fellow, Dave," he jeered. "I've seen them as would have grumbled a heap at digging up that sack, and then loaning me their horse to carry it whilst they walked. But you're that cheerful. My own brother wouldn't have been so kind."

Dingwell grunted sulkily. He may have felt cheerful, but he did not look it. The pudgy round body of Fox shook with silent laughter.

"Kind is the word, Dave. Honest, I hate to put myself under obligations to you like this. If I hadn't seen with my own eyes how you was feeling the need of them health exercises, I couldn't let you force your bronc on me. But this little walk will do you a lot of good. It ain't far. My horse is up there in the pines."

"What are you going to do with me?" growled the defeated man over his shoulder.

"Do with you?" The voice of Fox registered amiable surprise. "Why, I am going to ask you to go up to the horse ranch with me so that the boys can thank you proper for digging up the gold."

Directly in front of them a spur of the range jutted out to meet the brown foothills. Back of this, forty miles as the crow flies, nestled a mountain park surrounded by peaks. In it was the Rutherford horse ranch. Few men traveled to it, and these by little-used trails. Of those who frequented them, some were night riders. They carried a price on their heads, fugitives from localities where the arm of the law reached more surely.

Through the dry brittle grass the man on horseback followed Dingwell to the scant pines where his cowpony was tethered. Fox dismounted and stood over his captive while the latter transferred the gunnysack and its contents to the other saddle. Never for an instant did the little spy let the other man close enough to pounce upon him. Even though Dingwell was cowed, Chet proposed to play it safe. Not till he was in the saddle himself did he let his prisoner mount.

Instantly Dave's cowpony went into the air.

"Whoa, you Teddy! What's the matter with you?"

cried the owner of the horse angrily. "Quit your two-stepping, can't you?"

The animal had been gentle enough all day, but now a devil of unrest seemed to have entered it. The sound of trampling hoofs thudded on the hard, sun-baked earth as the bronco came down like a pile-driver, camel-backed, with legs stiff and unjointed. Skyward it flung itself again, whirled in the air, and jarred down at an angle. Wildly flapped the arms of the cattleman. The quirt, wrong end to, danced up and down clutched in his flying fist. Each moment it looked as if Mr. Dingwell would take the dust.

The fat stomach of Fox shook with mirth. "Go it, you buckaroo," he shouted. "You got him pulling leather. Sunfish, you pie-faced cayuse."

The horse in its lunges pounded closer. Fox backed away, momentarily alarmed. "Here—you, hold your brute off. It'll be on top of me in a minute," he screamed.

Apparently Dingwell had lost all control of the bucker. Somehow he still stuck to the saddle, by luck rather than skill it appeared. His arms, working like windmills, went up as Teddy shot into the air again. The humpbacked weaver came down close to the other horse. At the same instant Dingwell's loose arm grew rigid and the loaded end of the quirt dropped on the head of Fox.

The body of Fox relaxed and the rifle slid from his nerveless fingers. Teddy stopped bucking as if a spring had been touched. Dingwell was on his own feet before the other knew what had happened. His long arm plucked the little man from the saddle as if he had been a child.

Still jarred by the blow, Fox looked up with a ludicrous expression on his fat face. His mind was not yet adjusted to what had taken place.

"I told you to keep the brute away," he complained querulously. "Now, see what you've done."

Dave grinned. "Looks like I spilled your apple cart. No, don't bother about that gun. I'll take care of it for you. Much obliged."

Chet's face registered complex emotion. Incredulity struggled with resentment. "You made that horse buck on purpose," he charged.

"You're certainly a whiz, Chet," drawled the cattleman.

"And that business of being sore at yourself and ashamed was all a bluff. You were laying back to trick me," went on Fox venomously.

"How did you guess it? Well, don't you care. We're born to trouble as the sparks fly upward. As for man, his days are as grass. He diggeth a pit and falleth into it his own self. Likewise he digs a hole and buries gold, but behold, another guy finds it. See Second Ananias, fourteen, twelve."

"That's how you show your gratitude, is it? I might 'a' shot you safe and comfortable from the mesquite and saved a lot of trouble."

"I don't wonder you're disgusted, Chet. But be an optimist. I might 'a' busted you high and wide with that quirt instead of giving you a nice little easy tap that just did the business. There's no manner of use being regretful over past mistakes," Dave told him cheerfully.

"It's easy enough for you to say that," groaned Fox, his

hand to an aching head. "But I didn't lambaste you one on the nut. Anyhow, you've won out."

"I had won out all the time, only I hadn't pulled it off yet," Dingwell explained with a grin. "You didn't think I was going up to the horse ranch with you meek and humble, did you? But we can talk while we ride. I got to hustle back to Battle Butte and turn in this sack to the sheriff so as I can claim the reward. Hate to trouble you, Chet, but I'll have to ask you to transfer that gunnysack back to Teddy. He's through bucking for to-day, I shouldn't wonder."

Sourly Fox did as he was told. Then, still under orders, he mounted his own horse and rode back with his former prisoner to the park. Dingwell gathered up the rifle and revolver that had been left at the edge of the aspen grove and headed the horses for Battle Butte.

"We'll move lively, Chet," he said. "It will be night first thing we know."

Chet Fox was no fool. He could see how carefully Dingwell had built up the situation for his coup, and he began at once laying the groundwork for his own escape. There was in his mind no intention of trying to recover the gold himself, but if he could get away in time to let the Rutherfords know the situation, he knew that Dave would have an uneasy life of it.

" 'Course I was joking about shooting you up from the mesquite, Dave," he explained as the horses climbed the trail from the park. "I ain't got a thing against you—nothing a-tall. Besides, I'm a law-abiding citizen. I don't hold with this here gunman business. I never was a killer, and I don't aim to begin now."

"Sure, I know how tender-hearted you are, Chet. I'm that way, too. I'm awful sorry for myself when I get in trouble. That's why I tapped you on the cocoanut with the end of my quirt. That's why I'd let you have about three bullets from old Tried and True here right in the back if you tried to make your getaway. But, as you say, I haven't a thing against you. I'll promise you one of the nicest funerals Washington County ever had."

The little man laughed feebly. "You will have your joke, Dave, but I know mighty well you wouldn't shoot me. You got no legal right to detain me."

"I'd have to wrastle that out with the coroner afterward, I expect," replied Dingwell casually. "Not thinking of leaving me, are you?"

"Oh, no! No. Not at all. I was just kinder talking."

It was seven miles from Lonesome Park to Battle Butte. Fox kept up a kind of ingratiating whine whenever the road was so rough that the horses had to fall into a walk. He was not sure whether when it came to the pinch he could summon nerve to try a bolt, but he laid himself out to establish friendly relations. Dingwell, reading him like a primer, cocked a merry eye at the man and grinned.

About a mile from Battle Butte they caught up with another rider, a young woman of perhaps twenty. The dark, handsome face that turned to see who was coming would have been a very attractive one except for its look of sulky rebellion. From the mop of black hair tendrils had escaped and brushed the wet cheeks flushed by the sting of the rain. The girl rode splendidly. Even the slicker that she wore could not disguise the flat back and the erect carriage of the slender body.

Dingwell lifted his hat. "Good-evenin', Miss Rutherford."

She nodded curtly. Her intelligent eyes passed from his to those of Fox. A question and an answer, neither of them in words, flashed forth and back between Beulah Rutherford and the little man.

Dave took a hand in the line-up as they fell into place beside each other. "Hold on, Fox. You keep to the left of the road. I'll ride next you with Miss Rutherford on my right." He explained to the girl with genial mockery his reason. "Chet and I are such *tillicums* we hate to let any one get between us."

Bluntly the girl spoke out. "What's the matter?"

The cattleman lifted his eyebrows in amused surprise. "Why, nothing at all, I reckon. There's nothing the matter, is there, Chet?"

"I've got an engagement to meet your father and he won't let me go," blurted out Fox.

"When did you make that hurry-up appointment, Chet?" laughed Dingwell. "You didn't seem in no manner of hurry when you was lying in the mesquite back there at Lonesome Park."

"You've got no business to keep him here. He can go if he wants to," flashed the young woman.

"You hear that, Chet. You can go if you want to," murmured Dave with good-natured irony.

"Said he'd shoot me in the back if I hit the trail any faster," Fox snorted to the girl.

"He wouldn't dare," flamed Beulah Rutherford.

Her sultry eyes attacked Dingwell.

He smiled, not a whit disturbed. "You see how it is, Chet. Maybe I will; maybe I won't. Be a sport and you'll find out."

For a minute the three rode in silence except for the sound of the horses moving. Beulah did not fully understand the situation, but it was clear to her that somehow Dingwell was interfering with a plan of her people. Her untamed youth resented the high-handed way in which he seemed to be doing it. What right had he to hold Chet Fox a prisoner at the point of a rifle?

She asked a question flatly. "Have you got a warrant for Chet's arrest?"

"Only old Tried and True here." Dave patted the barrel of his weapon.

"You're not a deputy sheriff?"

"No-o. Not officially."

"What has Chet done?"

Dingwell regarded the other man humorously. "What have you done, Chet? You must 'a' broke some ordinance in that long career of disrespectability of yours. I reckon we'll put it that you obstructed traffic at Lonesome Park."

Miss Rutherford said no more. The rain had given way to a gentle mist. Presently she took off her slicker and held it on the left side of the saddle to fold. The cattleman leaned toward her to lend a hand.

"Lemme roll it up," he said.

"No, I can."

With the same motion the girl had learned in roping cattle she flung the slicker over his head. Her weight on the left stirrup, she threw her arms about him and drew the oil coat tight.

"Run, Chet!" she cried.

Fox was off like a flash.

Hampered by his rifle, Dave could use only one hand to free himself. The Rutherford girl clung as if her arms had been ropes of steel. Before he had shaken her off, the runaway was a hundred yards down the road galloping for dear life.

Dave raised his gun. Beulah struck the barrel down with her quirt. He lowered the rifle, turned to her, and smiled. His grin was rueful but friendly.

"You're a right enterprising young lady for a school-marm, but I wouldn't have shot Chet, anyhow. The circumstances don't warrant it."

She swung from the saddle and picked her coat out of the mud where it had fallen. Her lithe young figure was supple as that of a boy.

"You've spoiled my coat," she charged resentfully.

The injustice of this tickled him. "I'll buy you a new one when we get to town," he told her promptly.

Her angry dignity gave her another inch of height. "I'll attend to that, Mr. Dingwell. Suppose you ride on and leave me alone. I won't detain you."

"Meaning that she doesn't like your company, Dave," he mused aloud, eyes twinkling. "She seemed kinder fond of you, too, a minute ago."

Almost she stamped her foot. "Will you go? Or shall I?"

"Oh, I'm going, Miss Rutherford. If I wasn't such an aged, decrepit wreck I'd come up and be one of your scholars. Anyhow, I'm real glad to have met you. No, I can't stay longer. So sorry. Good-bye."

He cantered down the road in the same direction Fox had taken. It happened that he, too, wanted to be alone, for he had a problem to solve that would not wait. Fox had galloped in to warn the Rutherford gang that he had the gold. How long it would take him to round up two or three of them would depend on chance. Dave knew that they might be waiting for him before he reached town. He had to get rid of the treasure between that spot and town, or else he had to turn on his tired horse and try to escape to the hills. Into his mind popped a possible solution of the difficulty. It would depend on whether luck was for or against him. To dismount and hide the sack was impossible, both because Beulah Rutherford was on his heels and because the muddy road would show tracks where he had stopped. His plan was to hide it without leaving the saddle.

He did. At the outskirts of Battle Butte he crossed the bridge over Big Creek and deflected to the left. He swung up one street and down another beside which ran a small field of alfalfa on one side. A hundred yards beyond it he met another rider, a man called Slim Sanders, who worked for Buck Rutherford as a cowpuncher.

The two men exchanged nods without stopping. Apparently the news that Fox had brought was unknown to the cowboy. But Dingwell knew he was on his way to the Legal Tender Saloon, which was the hang-out of the Rutherford followers. In a few minutes Sanders would get his orders.

Dave rode to the house of Sheriff Sweeney. He learned there that the sheriff was downtown. Dingwell turned toward the business section of the town and rode down the main street. From a passer-by he learned that Sweeney had gone into the Legal Tender a few minutes before. In front of that saloon he dismounted.

Fifty yards down the street three men were walking toward him. He recognized them as Buck Rutherford, Sanders, and Chet Fox. The little man walked between the other two and told his story excitedly. Dingwell did not wait for them. He had something he wanted to tell Sweeney and he passed at once into the saloon.

CHAPTER 3

THE OLD-TIMER SITS INTO A BIG GAME

The room into which Dingwell had stepped was as large as a public dance-hall. Scattered in one part or another of it, singly or in groups, were fifty or sixty men. In front, to the right, was the bar, where some cowmen and prospectors were lined up before a counter upon which were bottles and glasses. A bartender in a white linen jacket was polishing the walnut top with a cloth.

Dave shook his head in answer to the invitation to drink that came to him at once. Casually he chatted with acquaintances as he worked his way toward the rear. This part of the room was a gambling resort. Among the various methods of separating the prodigal from his money were roulette, faro, keno, chuckaluck, and poker tables. Around these a motley assemblage was gathered. Rich cattlemen brushed shoulders with the outlaws who were rustling their calves. Mexicans without a nickel stood side by side with Eastern consumptives out for their health. Chinese laundrymen played the wheel beside miners and cowpunchers. Stolid, wooden-faced Indians in blankets from the reservation watched the turbid life of the Southwest as it eddied around them. The new West was jostling the old West into the background, but here the vivid life of the frontier was making its last stand.

By the time that Dave had made a tour of two thirds of the room he knew that Sheriff Sweeney was not among those present. His inquiries brought out the fact that he must have just left. Dingwell sauntered toward the door, intending to follow him, but what he saw there changed his mind. Buck Rutherford and Slim Sanders were lounging together at one end of the bar. It took no detective to understand that they were watching the door. A glance to the rear showed Dave two more Rutherfords at the back exit. That he would have company in case he left was a safe guess.

The cattleman chuckled. The little devils of mischief already mentioned danced in his eyes. If they were waiting for him to go, he would see that they had a long session of it. Dave was in no hurry. The night was young yet, and in any case the Legal Tender never closed. The key had been thrown away ten years before. He could sit it out as long as the Rutherfords could.

Dingwell was confident no move would be made against him in public. The sentiment of the community had developed since that distant day when the Rutherford gang had shot down Jack Beaudry in open daylight. Deviltry had to be done under cover now. Moreover,

Dave was in the peculiar situation of advantage that the outlaws could not kill him until they knew where he had hidden the gold. So far as the Rutherfords went, he was just now the goose that laid the golden egg.

He stood chatting with another cattleman for a few moments, then drifted back to the rear of the hall again. Underneath an elk's head with magnificent antlers a party sat around a table playing draw poker with a skinned deck. Two of them were wall-eyed strangers whom Dingwell guessed to be professional tinhorns. Another ran a curio store in town. The fourth was Dan Meldrum, one of the toughest crooks in the county. Nineteen years ago Sheriff Beaudry had sent him to the penitentiary for rustling calves. The fifth player sat next to the wall. He was a large, broad-shouldered man close to fifty. His face had the weather-beaten look of confidence that comes to an outdoor Westerner used to leading others.

While Dave was moving past this table, he noticed that Chet Fox was whispering in the ear of the man next the wall. The poker-player nodded, and at the same moment his glance met that of Dingwell. The gray eyes of the big fellow narrowed and grew chill. Fox, starting to move away, recognized the cattleman from whom he had escaped half an hour before. Taken by surprise, the little spy looked guilty as an urchin caught stealing apples.

It took no clairvoyant to divine what the subject of that whispered colloquy had been. The cheerful grin of Dave included impartially Fox, Meldrum, and the player beneath the elk's head.

The ex-convict spoke first. "Come back to sit in our game, Dave?" he jeered.

Dingwell understood that this was a challenge. It was impossible to look on the ugly, lupine face of the man, marked by the ravages of forty years of vice and unbridled passion, without knowing that he was ready for trouble now. But Meldrum was a mere detail of a situation piquant enough even for so light-hearted a son of the Rockies as this cattleman. Dave had already invited himself into a far bigger game of the Rutherford clan than this. Moreover, just now he was so far ahead that he had cleared the table of all the stakes. Meldrum knew this. So did Hal Rutherford, the big man sitting next the wall. What would be their next move? Perhaps if he joined them he would find out. This course held its dangers, but long experience had taught him that to walk through besetting perils was less risk than to run from them.

"If that's an invitation, Dan, you're on," he answered gayly. "Just a minute, and I'll join you. I want to send a message to Sweeney."

Without even looking at Meldrum to see the effect of this, Dave beckoned a Mexican standing near. "Tell the sheriff I want to see him here *pronto.* You win a dollar if he is back within an hour."

The Mexican disappeared. Fox followed him.

The cattleman drew in his chair and was introduced to the two strangers. The quick, searching look he gave each confirmed his first impression. These men were professional gamblers. It occurred to him that they had made a singularly poor choice of victims in Dan Meldrum and Hal Rutherford. Either of them would reach for his gun at the first evidence of crooked play.

No man in Battle Butte was a better poker psychologist than Dingwell, but to-night cards did not interest him. He was playing a bigger game. His subconscious mind was alert for developments. Since only his surface attention was given to poker he played close.

While Rutherford dealt the cards he talked at Dave. "So you're expecting Sweeney, are you? Been having trouble with any one?"

"Or expect to have any?" interjected Meldrum, insolence in his shifty pig eyes.

"No, not looking for any," answered Dingwell amiably. "Fact is, I was prospecting around Lonesome Park and found a gold mine. Looks good, so I thought I'd tell Sweeney about it. . . . Up to me? I've got openers." He pushed chips to the center of the table.

Rutherford also pushed chips forward. "I'll trail along. . . . You got an idea of taking in Sweeney as a partner? I'm looking for a good investment. *It would pay you to take me in rather than Sweeney.*"

Three of those at the table accepted this talk at its face value. They did not sense the tension underneath the apparently casual give-and-take. Two of them stayed and called for cards. But Dave understood that he had been offered a compromise. Rutherford had proposed to divide the gold stolen from the express car, and the proffer carried with it a threat in case of refusal.

"Two when you get to me. . . . No, I reckon I'll stick to the sheriff. I've kinda arranged the deal."

As Rutherford slid two cards across to him the eyes of the men met. "Call it off. Sweeney is not the kind of a partner to stay with you to the finish if your luck turns bad. When I give my word I go through."

Dingwell looked at his cards. "Check to the pat hand. . . . Point is, Hal, that I don't expect my luck to turn bad."

"Hmp! Go in with Sweeney and you'll have bad luck all right. *I'll promise you that.* Better talk this over with me and put a deal through." He rapped on the table to show that he too passed without betting.

The curio dealer checked and entered a mild protest. "Is this a poker game or a *conversazione,* gentlemen? It's stuck with Meldrum. I reckon he's off in Lonesome Park gold-mining the way he's been listening."

Meldrum brought his attention back to the game and bet his pat hand. Dave called. After a moment's hesitation Rutherford threw down his cards.

"There's such a thing as pushing your luck too far," he commented. "Now, take old man Crawford. He was mightily tickled when his brother Jim left him the Frying Pan Ranch. But that wasn't good enough as it stood. He had to try to better it by marrying the Swede hash-slinger from Los Angeles. Later she fed him arsenic in his coffee. A man's a fool to overplay his luck."

At the showdown Meldrum disclosed a four-card flush and the cattleman three jacks.

As Dave raked in the pot he answered Rutherford casually. "Still, he hadn't ought to underplay it either. The other fellow may be out on a limb."

"Say, is it any of your business how I play my cards?" demanded Meldrum, thrusting his chin toward Dingwell.

"Absolutely none," replied Dave evenly.

"Cut that out, Dan," ordered Rutherford curtly.

The ex-convict mumbled something into his beard, but subsided.

Two hours had slipped away before Dingwell commented on the fact that the sheriff had not arrived. He did not voice his suspicion that the Mexican had been intercepted by the Rutherfords.

"Looks like Sweeney didn't get my message," he said lazily. "You never can tell when a Mexican is going to get too tired to travel farther."

"Better hook up with me on that gold-mine proposition, Dave," Hal Rutherford suggested again.

"No, I reckon not, Hal. Much obliged, just the same."

Dave began to watch the game more closely. There were points about it worth noticing. For one thing, the two strangers had a habit of getting the others into a pot and cross-raising them exasperatingly. If Dave had kept even, it was only because he refused to be drawn into inviting pots when either of the strangers was dealing. He observed that though they claimed not to have met each other before there was team work in their play. Moreover, the yellow and blue chips were mostly piled up in front of them, while Meldrum, Rutherford, and the curio dealer had all bought several times. Dave waited until his doubts of crooked work became certainty before he moved.

"The game's framed. Blair has rung in a cold deck on us. He and Smith are playing in cahoots."

Dingwell had risen. His hands rested on the table as an assurance that he did not mean to back up his charge with a gunplay unless it became necessary.

The man who called himself Blair wasted no words in

denial. His right hand slid toward his hip pocket. Simultaneously the fingers of Dave's left hand knotted to a fist, his arm jolted forward, and the bony knuckles collided with the jaw of the tinhorn. The body of the cattleman had not moved. There seemed no special effort in the blow, but Blair went backward in his chair heels over head. The man writhed on the floor, turned over, and lay still.

From the moment that he had launched his blow Dave wasted no more attention on Blair. His eyes fastened upon Smith. The man made a motion to rise.

"Don't you," advised the cattleman gently. "Not till I say so, Mr. Smith. There's no manner of hurry a-tall. Meldrum, see what he's got in his right-hand pocket. Better not object, Smith, unless you want to ride at your own funeral."

Meldrum drew from the man's pocket a pack of cards.

"I thought so. They've been switching decks on us. The one we're playing with is marked. Run your finger over the ace of clubs there, Hal. . . . How about it?"

"Pin-pricked," announced Rutherford.

"And they've garnered in most of the chips. What do you think?"

"That I'll beat both their heads off," cut in Meldrum, purple with rage.

"Not necessary, Dan," vetoed Dingwell. "We'll shear the wolves. Each of you help yourself to chips equal to the amount you have lost. . . . Now, Mr. Smith, you and your partner will dig up one hundred and ninety-three dollars for these gentlemen."

"Why?" sputtered Smith. "It's all a frame-up. We've been playing a straight game. But say we haven't. They have got their chips back. Let them cash in to the house. What more do you want?"

"One hundred and ninety-three dollars. I thought I mentioned that already. You tried to rob these men of that amount, but you didn't get away with it. Now you'll rob yourself of just the same sum. Frisk yourself, Mr. Smith."

"Not on your life I won't. It . . . it's an outrage. It's robbery. I'll not stand for it." His words were brave, but the voice of the man quavered. The bulbous, fishy eyes of the cheat wavered before the implacable ones of the cattleman.

"Come through."

The gambler's gaze passed around the table and found no help from the men he had been robbing. A crowd was beginning to gather. Swiftly he decided to pay forfeit and get out while there was still time. He drew a roll of bills from his pocket and with trembling fingers counted out the sum named. He shoved it across the table and rose.

"Now, take your friend and both of you hit the trail out of town," ordered the cattleman.

Blair had by this time got to his feet and was leaning stupidly on a chair. His companion helped him from the room. At the door he turned and glared at Dingwell.

"You're going to pay for this—and pay big," he spat out, his voice shaking with rage.

"Oh, that's all right," answered Dingwell easily.

The game broke up. Rutherford nodded a good-night to the cattleman and left with Meldrum. Presently Dave noticed that Buck and the rest of the clan had also gone. Only Slim Sanders was left, and he was playing the wheel.

"Time to hit the hay," Dave yawned.

The bartender called "Good-night" as Dingwell went out of the swinging doors. He said afterward that he thought he heard the sound of scuffling and smothered voices outside. But his interest in the matter did not take him as far as the door to find out if anything was wrong.

CHAPTER 4

ROYAL BEAUDRY HEARS A CALL

A bow-legged little man with the spurs still jingling on his heels sauntered down one side of the old plaza. He passed a train of fagot-laden burros in charge of two Mexican boys from Tesuque, the sides and back of each diminished mule so packed with firewood that it was a comical caricature of a beruffed Elizabethan dame. Into the plaza narrow, twisted streets of adobe rambled carelessly. One of these led to the San Miguel Mission, said to be the oldest church in the United States.

An entire side of the square was occupied by a long, one-story adobe structure. This was the Governor's Palace. For three hundred years it had been the seat of turbulent and tragic history. Its solid walls had withstood many a siege and had stifled the cries of dozens of tortured prisoners. The mail-clad Spanish explorers Penelosa and De Salivar had from here set out across the desert on their search for gold and glory. In one of its rooms the last Mexican governor had dictated his defiance to General Kearny just before the Stars and Stripes fluttered from its flagpole. The Spaniard, the Indian, the

Mexican, and the American in turn had written here in action the romance of the Southwest.

The little man was of the outdoors. His soft gray creased hat, the sun-tan on his face and neck, the direct steadiness of the blue eyes with the fine lines at the corners, were evidence enough even if he had not carried in the wrinkles of his corduroy suit about seven pounds of white powdered New Mexico.

He strolled down the sidewalk in front of the Palace, the while he chewed tobacco absent-mindedly. There was something very much on his mind, so that it was by chance alone that his eye lit on a new tin sign tacked to the wall. He squinted at it incredulously. His mind digested the information it contained while his jaws worked steadily.

The sign read:—

DESPACHO

DE

ROYAL BEAUDRY, LICENCIADO

For those who preferred another language, a second announcement appeared below the first:—

ROYAL BEAUDRY

ATTORNEY AT LAW

"Sure, and it must be the boy himself," said the

little man aloud.

He opened the door and walked in.

A young man sat reading with his heels crossed on the top of a desk. A large calf-bound volume was open before him, but the book in the hands of the youth looked less formidable. It bore the title, "Adventures of Sherlock Holmes." The budding lawyer flashed a startled glance at his caller and slid Dr. Watson's hero into an open drawer.

The visitor grinned and remarked with a just perceptible Irish accent: "'T is a good book. I've read it myself."

The embryo Blackstone blushed. "Say, are you a client?" he asked.

"No-o."

"Gee! I was afraid you were my first. I like your looks. I'd hate for you to have the bad luck to get me for your lawyer." He laughed, boyishly. There was a very engaging quality about his candor.

The Irishman shot an abrupt question at him. "Are you John Beaudry's son—him that was fighting sheriff of Washington County twenty years ago?"

A hint of apprehension flickered into the eyes of the young man. "Yes," he said.

"Your father was a gr-reat man, the gamest officer that ever the Big Creek country saw. Me name is Patrick Ryan."

"Glad to meet any friend of my father, Mr. Ryan." Roy Beaudry offered his hand. His fine eyes glowed.

"Wait," warned the little cowpuncher grimly. "I'm no liar, whativer else I've been. Mebbe you'll be glad you've met me—an' mebbe you won't. First off, I was no friend of your father. I trailed with the Rutherford outfit them days. It's all long past and I'll tell youse straight that he just missed me in the round-up that sent two of our bunch to the pen."

In the heart of young Beaudry a chill premonition of evil stirred. His hand fell limply. Why had this man come out of the dead past to seek him? His panic-stricken eyes clung as though fascinated to those of Ryan.

"Do you mean . . . that you were a rustler?"

Ryan looked full at him. "You've said it. I was a wild young colt thim days, full of the divil and all. But remimber this. I held no grudge at Jack Beaudry. That's what he was elected for—to put me and my sort out of business. Why should I hate him because he was man enough to do it?"

"That's not what some of your friends thought."

"You're right, worse luck. I was out on the range when it happened. I'll say this for Hal Rutherford. He was full of bad whiskey when your father was murdered. . . . But that ended it for me. I broke with the Huerfano gang outfit and I've run straight iver since."

"Why have you come to me? What do you want?" asked the young lawyer, his throat dry.

"I need your help."

"What for? Why should I give it? I don't know you."

"It's not for mysilf that I want it. There's a friend of your father in trouble. When I saw the sign with your name on it I came in to tell you."

"What sort of trouble?"

"That's a long story. Did you iver hear of Dave Dingwell?"

"Yes. I've never met him, but he put me through law school."

"Howcome that?"

"I was living in Denver with my aunt. A letter came from Mr. Dingwell offering to pay the expenses of my education. He said he owed that much to my father."

"Well, then, Dave Dingwell has disappeared off the earth."

"What do you mean—disappeared?" asked Roy.

"He walked out of the Legal Tender Saloon one night and no friend of his has seen him since. That was last Tuesday."

"Is that all? He may have gone hunting—or to Denver—or Los Angeles."

"No, he didn't do any one of the three. He was either murdered or else hid out in the hills by them that had a reason for it."

"Do you suspect some one?"

"I do," answered Ryan promptly. "If he was killed, two tinhorn gamblers did it. If he's under guard in the hills, the Rutherford gang have got him."

"The Rutherfords, the same ones that—?"

"The ver-ry same—Hal and Buck and a brood of young hellions they have raised."

"But why should they kidnap Mr. Dingwell? If they had anything against him, why wouldn't they kill him?"

"If the Rutherfords have got him it is because he knows something they want to know. Listen, and I'll tell you what I think."

The Irishman drew up a chair and told Beaudry the story of that night in the Legal Tender as far as he could piece it together. He had talked with one of the poker-players, the man that owned the curio store, and from him had gathered all he could remember of the talk between Dingwell and Rutherford.

"Get these points, lad," Ryan went on. "Dave comes to town from a long day's ride. He tells Rutherford that he has been prospecting and has found gold in Lonesome Park. Nothing to that. Dave is a cattleman, not a prospector. Rutherford knows that as well as I do. But he falls right in with Dingwell's story. He offers to go partners with Dave on his gold mine—keeps talking about it—insists on going in with him."

"I don't see anything in that," said Roy.

"You will presently. Keep it in mind that there wasn't any gold mine and couldn't have been. That talk was a blind to cover something else. Good enough. Now chew on this awhile. Dave sent a Mexican to bring the sheriff, but Sweeney didn't come. He explained that he wanted to go partners with Sweeney about this gold-mine proposition. If he was talking about a real gold mine, that is teetotally unreasonable. Nobody would pick Sweeney for a partner. He's a fathead and Dave worked against him before election. But Sweeney *is sheriff of Washington County*. Get that?"

"I suppose you mean that Dingwell had something on the Rutherfords and was going to turn them over to the law."

"You're getting warm, boy. Does the hold-up of the Pacific Flyer help you any?"

Roy drew a long breath of surprise. "You mean the Western Express robbery two weeks ago?"

"Sure I mean that. Say the Rutherford outfit did that job."

"And that Dingwell got evidence of it. But then they would kill him." The heart of the young man sank. He had a warm place in it for this unknown friend who had paid his law-school expenses.

"You're forgetting about the gold mine Dave claimed to have found in Lonesome Park. Suppose he was hunting strays and saw them cache their loot somewhere. Suppose he dug it up. Say they knew he had it, but didn't know where he had taken it. They couldn't kill him. They would have to hold him prisoner till they could make him tell where it was."

The young lawyer shook his head. "Too many *ifs*. Each one makes a weak joint in your argument. Put them all together and it is full of holes. Possible, but extremely improbable."

An eager excitement flashed in the blue eyes of the Irishman.

"You're looking at the thing wrong end to. Get a grip on your facts first. The Western Express Company was robbed of twenty thousand dollars and the robbers were run into the hills. The Rutherford outfit is the very gang to pull off that hold-up. Dave tells Hal Rutherford, the leader of the tribe, that he has sent for the sheriff. Hal tries to get him to call it off. Dave talks about a gold mine he has found and Rutherford tries to fix up a deal with him. There's no *if* about any of that, me young Sherlock Holmes."

"No, you've built up a case. But there's a stronger case already built for us, isn't there? Dingwell exposed the gamblers Blair and Smith, knocked one of them cold, made them dig up a lot of money, and drove them out of town. They left, swearing vengeance. He rides away, and he is never seen again. The natural assumption is that they lay in wait for him and killed him."

"Then where is the body?"

"Lying out in the cactus somewhere—or buried in the sand."

"That wouldn't be a bad guess—if it wasn't for another bit of testimony that came in to show that Dave was alive five hours after he left the Legal Tender. A sheepherder on the Creosote Flats heard the sound of horses' hoofs early next morning. He looked out of his tent and saw three horses. Two of the riders carried rifles. The third rode between them. He didn't carry any gun. They were a couple of hundred yards away and the herder didn't recognize any of the men. But it looked to him like the man without the gun was a prisoner."

"Well, what does that prove?"

"If the man in the middle was Dave—and that's the hunch I'm betting on to the limit—it lets out the tin-horns. Their play would be to kill and make a quick get-away. There wouldn't be any object in their taking a prisoner away off to the Flats. If this man was Dave, Blair and Smith are eliminated from the list of suspects. That leaves the Rutherfords."

"But you don't know that this was Dingwell."

"That's where you come in, me brave Sherlock. Dave's friends can't move to help him. You see, they're all known men. It might be the end of Dave if they lifted a finger. But you're not known to the Rutherfords. You slip in over Wagon Wheel Gap to Huerfano Park, pick up what you can, and come out to Battle Butte with your news."

"You mean—spy on them?"

"Of coorse."

"But what if they suspected me?"

"Then your heirs at law would collect the insurance," Ryan told him composedly.

Excuses poured out of young Beaudry one on top of another. "No, I can't go. I won't mix up in it. It's not my affair. Besides, I can't get away from my business."

"I see your business keeps you jumping," dryly commented the Irishman. "And you know best whether it's your affair."

Beaudry could have stood it better if the man had railed at him, if he had put up an argument to show why he must come to the aid of the friend who had helped him. This cool, contemptuous dismissal of him stung. He began to pace the room in rising excitement.

"I hate that country up there. I've got no use for it. It killed my mother just as surely as it did my father. I left there when I was a child, but I'll never forget that dreadful day seventeen years ago. Sometimes I wake in bed out of some devil's nightmare and live it over. Why should I go back to that bloody battleground? Hasn't it cost me enough already? It's easy for you to come and tell me to go to Huerfano Park—"

"Hold your horses, Mr. Beaudry. I'm not tellin' you to go. I've laid the facts before ye. Go or stay as you please."

"That's all very well," snapped back the young man. "But I know what you'll think of me if I don't go."

"What you'll think of yourself matters more. I haven't got to live with ye for forty years."

Roy Beaudry writhed. He was sensitive and high-strung. Temperamentally he coveted the good opinion of those about him. Moreover, he wanted to deserve it. No man had ever spoken to him in just the tone of this little Irish cowpuncher, who had come out of nowhere into his life and brought to him his first big problem for decision. Even though the man had confessed himself a rustler, the young lawyer could not escape his judgment. Pat Ryan might have ridden on many lawless trails in his youth, but the dynamic spark of self-respect still burned in his soul. He was a man, every inch of his five-foot three.

"I want to live at peace," the boy went on hotly. "Huerfano Park is still in the dark ages. I'm no gunman. I stand for law and order. This is the day of civilization. Why should I embroil myself with a lot of murderous outlaws when what I want is to sit here and make friends—?"

The Irishman hammered his fist on the table and exploded. "Then sit here, damn ye! But why the hell should any one want to make friends with a white-livered pup like you? I thought you was Jack Beaudry's son, but I'll niver believe it. Jack didn't sit on a padded chair and talk about law and order. By God, no! He went out with a six-gun and *made* them. No gamer, whiter man ever strapped a forty-four to his hip. *He* niver talked about what it would cost him to go through for his friends. He just went the limit without any guff."

Ryan jingled out of the room in hot scorn and left one

young peace advocate in a turmoil of emotion.

Young Beaudry did not need to discuss with himself the ethics of the situation. A clear call had come to him on behalf of the man who had been his best friend, even though he had never met him. He must answer that call, or he must turn his back on it. Sophistry would not help at all. There were no excuses his own mind would accept.

But Royal Beaudry had been timid from his childhood. He had inherited fear. The shadow of it had always stretched toward him. His cheeks burned with shame to recall that it had not been a week since he had looked under the bed at night before getting in to make sure nobody was hidden there. What was the use of blinking the truth? He was a born coward. It was the skeleton in the closet of his soul. His schooldays had been haunted by the ghost of dread. Never in his life had he played truant, though he had admired beyond measure the reckless little dare-devils who took their fun and paid for it. He had contrived to avoid fights with his mates and thrashings from the teachers. On the one occasion when public opinion had driven him to put up his fists, he had been saved from disgrace only because the bully against whom he had turned proved to be an arrant craven.

He remembered how he had been induced to go out and try for the football team at the university. His fellows knew him as a fair gymnast and a crack tennis player. He was muscular, well-built, and fast on his feet, almost perfectly put together for a halfback. On the second day of practice he had shirked a hard tackle, though it happened that nobody suspected the truth but himself. Next morning he turned in his suit with the plea that he had promised his aunt not to play.

Now trepidation was at his throat again, and there was no escape from a choice that would put a label on him. It had been his right to play football or not as he pleased. But this was different. A summons had come to his loyalty, to the fundamental manhood of him. If he left David Dingwell to his fate, he could never look at himself again in the glass without knowing that he was facing a dastard.

The trouble was that he had too much imagination. As a child he had conjured dragons out of the darkness that had no existence except in his hectic fancy. So it was now. He had only to give his mind play to see himself helpless in the hands of the Rutherfords.

But he was essentially stanch and generous. Fate had played him a scurvy trick in making him a trembler, but he knew it was not in him to turn his back on Dingwell. No matter how much he might rebel and squirm he would have to come to time in the end.

After a wretched afternoon he hunted up Ryan at his hotel.

"When do you want me to start?" he asked sharply.

The little cowpuncher was sitting in the lobby reading a newspaper. He took one look at the harassed youth and jumped up.

"Say, you're all right. Put her there."

Royal's cold hand met the rough one of Ryan. The shrewd eyes of the Irishman judged the other.

"I knew youse couldn't be a quitter and John Beaudry's son," he continued. "Why, come to that, the sooner you start the quicker."

"I'll have to change my name."

"Sure you will. And you'd better peddle something—insurance, or lightning rods, or 'The Royal Gall'ry of Po'try 'n Art' or—"

"'Life of the James and Younger Brothers.' That ought to sell well with the Rutherfords," suggested Roy satirically, trying to rise to the occasion.

"Jess Tighe and Dan Meldrum don't need any pointers from the James Boys."

"Tighe and Meldrum—who are they?"

"Meldrum is a coyote your father trapped and sent to the pen. He's a bad actor for fair. And Tighe—well, if you put a hole in his head you'd blow out the brains of the Rutherford gang. For hiven's sake don't let Jess know who you are. All of sivinteen years he's been a cripple on crutches, an 't was your father that laid him up the day of his death. He's a rivingeful divil is Jess."

Beaudry made no comment. It seemed to him that his heart was of chilled lead.

CHAPTER 5

THE HILL GIRL

The Irish cowpuncher guided young Royal Beaudry through Wagon Wheel Gap himself. They traveled in the night, since it would not do for the two to be seen together. In the early morning Ryan left the young man and turned back toward Battle Butte. The way to Huerfano Park, even from here, was difficult to find, but Roy had a map drawn from memory by Pat.

"I'll not guarantee it," the little rider had cautioned. "It's been many a year since I was in to the park and maybe my memory is playing tricks. But it's the best I can do for you."

Beaudry spent the first half of the day in a pine grove far up in the hills. It would stir suspicion if he were seen on the road at dawn, for that would mean that he must have come through the Gap in the night. So he unsaddled and stretched himself on the sun-dappled ground for an hour or two's rest. He did not expect to sleep, even though he had been up all night. He was too uneasy in mind and his nerves were too taut.

But it was a perfect day of warm spring sunshine. He looked up into a blue unflecked sky. The tireless hum of insects made murmurous music all about him. The air was vocal with the notes of nesting birds. His eyes closed drowsily.

When he opened them again, the sun was high in the heavens. He saddled and took the trail. Within the hour he knew that he was lost. Either he had mistaken some of the landmarks of Ryan's sketchy map or else the cow-puncher had forgotten the lay of the country.

Still, Roy knew roughly the general direction of Huerfano Park. If he kept going he was bound to get nearer. Perhaps he might run into a road or meet some sheep-herder who would put him on the right way.

He was in the heart of the watershed where Big Creek heads. Occasionally from a hilltop he could see the peaks rising gaunt in front of him. Between him and them were many miles of tangled mesquite, wooded cañons, and hills innumerable. Somewhere among the recesses of these land waves Huerfano Park was hidden.

It was three o'clock by Royal's watch when he had worked to the top of a bluff which looked down upon a wooded valley. His eyes swept the landscape and came to rest upon an object moving slowly in the mesquite. He watched it incuriously, but his interest quickened when it came out of the bushes into a dry water-course and he discovered that the figure was that of a human being. The person walked with an odd, dragging limp. Presently he discerned that the traveler below was a woman and that she was pulling something after her. For perhaps fifty yards she would keep going and then would stop. Once she crouched down over her load.

Roy cupped his hands at his mouth and shouted. The figure straightened alertly and looked around. He called to her again. His voice must have reached her very faintly. She did not try to answer in words, but fired twice with a revolver. Evidently she had not yet seen him.

That there was something wrong Beaudry felt sure. He did not know what, nor did he waste any time speculating about it. The easiest descent to the valley was around the rear of the bluff, but Roy clambered down a heavily wooded gulch a little to the right. He saved time by going directly.

When Roy saw the woman again he was close upon her. She was stooped over something and her back and arms showed tension. At sound of his approach she flung up quickly the mass of inky black hair that had hidden her bent face. As she rose it became apparent that she was tall and slender, and that the clear complexion, just now at least, was quite without color.

Moving forward through the underbrush, Beaudry took stock of this dusky nymph with surprise. In her attitude was something wild and free and proud. It was as if she challenged his presence even though she had summoned him. Across his mind flashed the thought that this was woman primeval before the conventions of civilization had tamed her to its uses.

Her intent eyes watched him steadily as he came into the open.

"Who are you?" she demanded.

"I was on the bluff and saw you. I thought you were in trouble. You limped as if—"

He stopped, amazed. For the first time he saw that her foot was caught in a wolf trap. This explained the peculiarity of gait he had noticed from above. She had been dragging the heavy Newhouse trap and the clog with her as she walked. One glance at her face was enough to show how greatly she was suffering.

Fortunately she was wearing a small pair of high-heeled boots such as cowpunchers use, and the stiff leather had broken the shock of the blow from the steel jaws. Otherwise the force of the released spring must have shattered her ankle.

"I can't quite open the trap," she explained. "If you will help me—"

Roy put his weight on the springs and removed the pressure of the jaws. The girl drew out her numb leg. She straightened herself, swayed and clutched blindly at him. Next moment her body relaxed and she was unconscious in his arms.

He laid her on the moss and looked about for water. There was some in his canteen, but that was attached to the saddle on the top of the bluff. For present purposes it might as well have been at the North Pole. He could not leave her while she was like this. But since he had to be giving some first aid, he drew from her foot the boot that had been in the steel trap, so as to relieve the ankle.

Her eyelids fluttered, she gave a deep sigh, and looked with a perplexed doubt upon the world to which she had just returned.

"You fainted," Roy told her by way of explanation.

The young woman winced and looked at her foot. The angry color flushed into her cheeks. Her annoyance was at herself, but she visited it upon him.

"Who told you to take off my boot?"

"I thought it might help the pain."

She snatched up the boot and started to pull it on, but gave this up with a long breath that was almost a groan.

"I'm a nice kind of a baby," she jeered.

"It must hurt like sixty," he ventured. Then, after momentary hesitation: "You'd better let me bind up your ankle. I have water in my canteen. I'll run up and get some as soon as I'm through."

There was something of sullen suspicion in the glance her dark eyes flashed at him.

"You can get me water if you want to," she told him, a little ungraciously.

He understood that his offer to tie up the ankle had been refused. When he returned with his horse twenty minutes later, he knew why she had let him go for the water. It had been the easiest way to get rid of him for the time. The fat bulge beneath her stocking showed that she had taken advantage of his absence to bind the bruised leg herself.

"Is it better now—less painful?" he asked.

She dismissed his sympathy with a curt little nod. "I'm the biggest fool in Washington County. We've been setting traps for wolves. They've been getting our lambs. I jumped off my horse right into this one. Blacky is a skittish colt and when the trap went off, he bolted."

He smiled a little at the disgust she heaped upon herself.

"You'll have to ride my horse to your home. How far is it?"

"Five miles, maybe." The girl looked at her ankle resentfully. It was plain that she did not relish the idea of being under obligations to him. But to attempt to walk so far was out of the question. Even now when she was not using the foot she suffered a good deal of pain.

"Cornell isn't a bit skittish. He's an old plug. You'll find his gait easy," Beaudry told her.

If she had not wanted to keep her weight from the wounded ankle, she would have rejected scornfully his offer to help her mount, for she was used to flinging her lithe body into the saddle as easily as her brothers did. The girl had read in books of men aiding women to reach their seat on the back of a horse, but she had not the least idea how the thing was done. Because of her ignorance she was embarrassed. The result was that they boggled the business, and it was only at the third attempt that he got her on as gracefully as if she had been a sack of meal.

"Sorry. I'm awfully awkward," he apologized.

Again an angry flush stained her cheeks. The stupidity had been hers, not his. She resented it that he was ready to take the blame, read into his manner a condescension he did not at all feel.

"I know whose fault it was. I'm not a fool," she snapped brusquely.

It added to her irritation at making such an exhibition of clumsiness that she was one of the best horsewomen in the Territory. Her life had been an outdoor one, and she had stuck to the saddle on the back of many an outlaw bronco without pulling leather. There were many things of which she knew nothing. The ways of sophisticated women, the conventions of society, were alien to her life. She was mountain-bred, brought up among men, an outcast even from the better class of Battle Butte. But the life of the ranch she knew. That this soft-cheeked boy from town should think she did not know how to get on a horse was a little too humiliating. Some day, if she ever got a chance, she would let him see her vault into the saddle without touching the stirrups.

The young man walking beside the horse might still be smooth-cheeked, but he had the muscles of an athlete. He took the hills with a light, springy step and breathed easily after stiff climbing. His mind was busy making out what manner of girl this was. She was new to his experience. He had met none like her. That she was a proud, sulky creature he could easily guess from her quickness at taking offense. She resented even the appearance of being ridiculous. Her acceptance of his favors carried always the implication that she hated him for offering them. It was a safe guess that back of those flashing eyes were a passionate temper and an imperious will.

It was evident that she knew the country as a teacher knows the primer through which she leads her children. In daylight or in darkness, with or without a trail, she could have followed almost an air-line to the ranch. The paths she took wound in and out through unsuspected gorges and over divides that only goats or cowponies could have safely scrambled up and down. Hidden pockets had been cached here so profusely by nature that the country was a maze. A man might have found safety from pursuit in one of these for a lifetime if he had been provisioned.

"Where were you going when you found me?" the young woman asked.

"Up to the mountain ranches of Big Creek. I was lost, so we ought to put it that you found me," Beaudry answered with the flash of a pleasant smile.

"What are you going to do up there?" Her keen suspicious eyes watched him warily.

"Sell windmills if I can. I've got the best proposition on the market."

"Why do you come away up here? Don't you know that the Big Creek headwaters are off the map?"

"That's it exactly," he replied. "I expect no agents get up here. It's too hard to get in. I ought to be able to sell a whole lot easier than if I took the valleys." He laughed a little, by way of taking her into his confidence. "I'll tell the ranchers that if they buy my windmills it will put Big Creek on the map."

"They won't buy them," she added with a sudden flare of temper. "This country up here is fifty years behind the times. It doesn't want to be modern."

Over a boulder bed, by rock fissures, they came at last to a sword gash in the top of the world. It cleft a passage through the range to another gorge, at the foot of which lay a mountain park dotted with ranch buildings. On every side the valley was hemmed in by giant peaks.

"Huerfano Park?" he asked.

"Yes."

"You live here?"

"Yes." She pointed to a group of buildings to the left. "That is my father's place. They call it the 'Horse Ranch.'"

He turned startled eyes upon her. "Then you are—?"

"Beulah Rutherford, the daughter of Hal Rutherford."

CHAPTER 6

"CHEROKEE STREET"

She was the first to break the silence after her announcement.

"What's the matter? You look as if you had seen a ghost."

He had. The ghost of a dreadful day had leaped at him out of the past. Men on murder bent were riding down the street toward their victim. At the head of that company rode *her* father; the one they were about to kill was *his*. A wave of sickness shuddered through him.

"It—it's my heart," he answered in a smothered voice.

"Sometimes it acts queer. I'll be all right in a minute."

The young woman drew the horse to a halt and looked down at him. Her eyes, for the first time since they had met, registered concern.

"The altitude, probably. We're over nine thousand feet high. You're not used to walking in the clouds. We'll rest here."

She swung from the saddle and trailed the reins.

"Sit down," the girl ordered after she had seated herself tailor-fashion on the moss.

Reluctantly he did as he was told. He clenched his teeth in a cold rage at himself. Unless he conquered that habit of flying into panic at every crisis, he was lost.

Beulah leaned forward and plucked an anemone blossom from a rock cranny. "Isn't it wonderful how brave they are? You wouldn't think they would have courage to grow up so fine and delicate among the rocks without any soil to feed them."

Often, in the days that followed, he thought of what she had said about the anemones and applied it to herself. She, too, had grown up among the rocks spiritually. He could see the effect of the barren soil in her suspicious and unfriendly attitude toward life. There was in her manner a resentment at fate, a bitterness that no girl of her years should have felt. In her wary eyes he read distrust of him. Was it because she was the product of heredity and environment? Her people had outlawed themselves from society. They had lived with their hands against the world of settled order. She could not escape the law that their turbulent sins must be visited upon her.

Young Beaudry followed the lead she had given him.

"Yes, that is the most amazing thing in life—that no matter how poor the soil and how bad the conditions fine and lovely things grow up everywhere."

The sardonic smile on her dark face mocked him. "You find a sermon in it, do you?"

"Don't you?"

She plucked the wild flower out by the roots. "It struggles—and struggles—and blooms for a day—and withers. What's the use?" she demanded, almost savagely. Then, before he could answer, the girl closed the door she had opened for him. "We must be moving. The sun has already set in the valley."

His glances swept the park below. Heavily wooded gulches pushed down from the roots of the mountains that girt Huerfano to meet the fences of the ranchers. The cliffs rose sheer and bleak. The panorama was a wild and primitive one. It suggested to the troubled mind of the young man an eagle's nest built far up in the crags from which the great bird could swoop down upon its victims. He carried the figure farther. Were these hillmen eagles, hawks, and vultures? And was he beside them only a tomtit? He wished he knew.

"Were you born here?" he asked, his thoughts jumping back to the girl beside him.

"Yes."

"And you've always lived here?"

"Except for one year when I went away to school."

"Where?"

"To Denver."

The thing he was thinking jumped into words almost unconsciously.

"Do you like it here?"

"Like it?" Her dusky eyes stabbed at him. "What does it matter whether I like it? I have to live here, don't I?"

The swift parry and thrust of the girl was almost ferocious.

"I oughtn't to have put it that way," he apologized. "What I meant was, did you like your year outside at school?"

Abruptly she rose. "We'll be going. You ride down. My foot is all right now."

"I wouldn't think of it," he answered promptly. "You might injure yourself for life."

"I tell you I'm all right," she said, impatience in her voice.

To prove her claim she limped a few yards slowly. In spite of a stubborn will the girl's breath came raggedly. Beaudry caught the bridle of the horse and followed her.

"Don't please. You might hurt yourself," he urged.

She nodded. "All right. Bring the horse close to that big rock."

From the boulder she mounted without his help. Presently she asked a careless question.

"Why do you call him Cornell? Is it for the college?"

"Yes. I went to school there a year." He roused himself to answer with the proper degree of lightness. "At the ball games we barked in chorus a rhyme: 'Cornell I yell—yell—yell—Cornell.' That's how it is with this old plug. If I want to get anywhere before the day after tomorrow, I have to yell—yell—yell."

The young woman showed in a smile a row of white strong teeth. "I see. His real name is Day-After-To-

Morrow, but you call him Cornell for short. Why not just Corn? He would appreciate that, perhaps."

"You've christened him, Miss Rutherford. Corn he shall be, henceforth and forevermore."

They picked their way carefully down through the cañon and emerged from it into the open meadow. The road led plain and straight to the horse ranch. Just before they reached the house, a young man cantered up from the opposite direction.

He was a black-haired, dark young giant of about twenty-four. Before he turned to the girl, he looked her companion over casually and contemptuously.

"Hello, Boots! Where's your horse?" he asked.

"Bolted. Hasn't Blacky got home yet?"

"Don't know. Haven't been home. Get thrown?"

"No. Stepped into one of your wolf traps." She turned to include Beaudry. "This gentleman—Mr.—?"

Caught at a disadvantage, Roy groped wildly for the name he had chosen. His mind was a blank. At random he snatched for the first that came. It happened to be his old Denver address.

"Cherokee Street," he gasped.

Instantly he knew he had made a mistake.

"That's odd," Beulah said. "There's a street called Cherokee in Denver. Were you named for it?"

He lied, not very valiantly. "Yes, I—I think so. You see, I was born on it, and my parents—since their name was Street, anyhow,—thought it a sort of distinction to give me that name. I've never much liked it."

The girl spoke to the young man beside her. "Mr. Street helped me out of the trap and lent me his horse to get home. I hurt my leg." She proceeded to introductions. "Mr. Street, this is my brother, Jeff Rutherford."

Jeff nodded curtly. He happened to be dismounting, so he did not offer to shake hands. Over the back of the horse he looked at his sister's guest without comment. Again he seemed to dismiss him from his mind as of no importance. When he spoke, it was to Beulah.

"That's a fool business—stepping into wolf traps. How did you come to do it?"

"It doesn't matter how I did it."

"Hurt any?"

She swung from the saddle and limped a few steps. "Nothing to make any fuss about. Dad home?"

"Yep. Set the trap again after you sprung it, Boots?"

"No. Set your own traps," she flung over her shoulder. "This way, Mr. Street."

Roy followed her to the house and was ushered into a room where a young man sat cleaning a revolver with one leg thrown across a second chair. Tilted on the back of his head was a cowpuncher's pinched-in hat. He too had black hair and a black mustache. Like all the Rutherfords he was handsome after a fashion, though the debonair recklessness of his good looks offered a warning of temper.

" 'Lo, Boots," he greeted his sister, and fastened his black eyes on her guest.

Beaudry noticed that he did not take off his hat or lift his leg from the chair.

"Mr. Street, this is my brother Hal. I don't need to tell you that he hasn't been very well brought up."

Young Rutherford did not accept the hint. "My friends

take me as they find me, sis. Others can go to Guinea."

Beulah flushed with annoyance. She drew one of the gauntlets from her hand and with the fingers of it flipped the hat from the head of her brother. Simultaneously her foot pushed away the chair upon which his leg rested.

He jumped up, half inclined to be angry. After a moment he thought better of it, and grinned.

"I'm not the only member of the family shy on manners, Boots," he said. "What's the matter with you? Showing off before company?"

"I'd have a fine chance with you three young rowdies in the house," she retorted derisively. "Where's dad?"

As if in answer to her question the door opened to let in a big, middle-aged rancher with a fine shock of grizzled hair and heavy black eyebrows. Beulah went through the formula of introduction again, but without it Beaudry would have known this hawk-nosed man whose gaze bored into his. The hand he offered to Hal Rutherford was cold and clammy. A chill shiver passed through him.

The young woman went on swiftly to tell how her guest had rescued her from the wolf trap and walked home beside her while she rode his horse.

"I'll send for Doc Spindler and have him look at your ankle, honey," the father announced at once.

"Oh, it's all right—bruised up a bit—that's all," Beulah objected.

"We'll make sure, Boots. Slap a saddle on and ride for the Doc, Hal." When the young man had left the room, his father turned again to Roy. His arm gathered in the girl beside him. "We're sure a heap obliged to you, Mr.

Street. It was right lucky you happened along."

To see the father and daughter together was evidence enough of the strong affection that bound them. The tone in which he had spoken to his son had been brusque and crisp, but when he addressed her, his voice took on a softer inflection, his eyes betrayed the place she held in his heart.

The man looked what he was—the chief of a clan, the almost feudal leader of a tribe which lived outside the law. To deny him a certain nobility of appearance was impossible. Young Beaudry guessed that he was arrogant, but this lay hidden under a manner of bluff frankness. One did not need a second glance to see from whom the younger Rutherfords had inherited their dark, good looks. The family likeness was strong in all of them, but nature had taken her revenge for the anti-social life of the father. The boys had reverted toward savagery. They were elemental and undisciplined. This was, perhaps, true of Beulah also. There were moments when she suggested in the startled poise of her light body and the flash of her quick eyes a wild young creature of the forest set for flight. But in her case atavism manifested itself charmingly in the untamed grace of a rich young personality vital with life. It was an interesting speculation whether in twenty years she would develop into a harridan or a woman of unusual character.

The big living-room of the ranch house was a man's domain. A magnificent elk head decorated one of the walls. Upon the antlers rested a rifle and from one of the tines depended a belt with a six-shooter in its holster. A braided leather quirt lay on the table and beside it a spur one of the boys had brought in to be riveted. Tossed carelessly into one corner were a fishing rod and a creel. A shotgun and a pair of rubber waders occupied the corner diagonally opposite.

But there were evidences to show that Beulah had modified at least her environment. An upright piano and a music-rack were the most conspicuous. Upon the piano was a padded-covered gift copy of "Aurora Leigh." A similar one of "In Memoriam" lay on the mantel next to a photograph of the girl's dead mother framed in small shells. These were mementoes of Beulah's childhood. A good copy of Del Sarto's "John the Baptist" hanging from the wall and two or three recent novels offered an intimation that she was now beyond shell frames and padded-leather editions.

Miss Rutherford hobbled away to look after her ankle and to give orders for supper to the ranch cook. Conversation waned. The owner of the place invited Roy out to look over with him a new ram he had just imported from Galloway. The young man jumped at the chance. He knew as much about sheep as he did of Egyptian hieroglyphics, but he preferred to talk about the mange rather than his reasons for visiting Huerfano Park.

Just at present strangers were not welcome in the park. Rutherford himself was courteous on account of the service he had done Beulah, but the boys were frankly suspicious. Detectives of the express company had been poking about the hills. Was this young fellow who called himself Street a spy sent in by the Western? While Beaudry ate supper with the family, he felt himself under the close observation of four pairs of watchful eyes.

Afterward a young man rode into the ranch and another pair of eyes was added to those that took stock of the guest. Brad Charlton said he had come to see Ned Rutherford about a gun, but Ned's sister was the real reason for his call. This young man was something of a dandy. He wore a Chihuahua hat and the picturesque trappings with which the Southwest sometimes adorns itself. The fine workmanship of the saddle, bridle, and stirrups was noticeable. His silk handkerchief, shirt, and boots were of the best. There was in his movements an easy and graceful deliberation, but back of his slowness was a chill, wary strength.

Roy discovered shortly that Charlton was a local Admirable Crichton. He was known as a crack rider, a good roper, and a dead shot. Moreover, he had the reputation of being ready to fight at the drop of the hat. To the Rutherford boys he was a hero. Whether he was one also to Beulah her guest had not yet learned, but it took no wiseacre to guess that he wanted to be.

As soon as the eyes of Charlton and Beaudry met there was born between them an antagonism. Jealousy sharpened the suspicions of the young rancher. He was the sort of man that cannot brook rivalry. That the newcomer had been of assistance to Miss Rutherford was enough in itself to stir his doubts.

He set himself to verify them.

CHAPTER 7

JESS TIGHE SPINS A WEB

"Then you left Denver, did you?" asked Charlton suavely.

Roy laughed. "Yes, then I left Denver and went to college and shouted, 'Rah, rah, rah, Cornell.' In time I became a man and put away childish things. Can I sell you a windmill, Mr. Charlton, warranted to raise more water with less air pressure than any other in the market?"

"Been selling windmills long?" the rancher asked casually.

It was his ninth question in fifteen minutes. Beaudry knew that he was being cross-examined and his study of law had taught him that he had better stick to the truth so far as possible. He turned to Miss Rutherford.

"Your friend is bawling me out," he gayly pretended to whisper. "I never sold a windmill in my life. But I'm on my uppers. I've got a good proposition. This country needs the Dynamo Aermotor and I need the money. So I took the agency. I have learned a fifteen minutes' spiel. It gives seven reasons why Mr. Charlton will miss half the joy of life until he buys a Dynamo. Do you think he is a good prospect, Miss Rutherford?"

"Dad has been talking windmill," she said. "Sell him one."

"So has Jess Tighe," Charlton added. He turned to Jeff Rutherford. "Couldn't you take Mr. Street over to see Jess to-morrow morning?"

Jeff started promptly to decline, but as his friend's eyes met his he changed his mind. "I guess I could, maybe."

"I don't want to trouble you, Mr. Rutherford," objected Roy.

Something in the manner of Charlton annoyed Beulah. This young man was her guest. She did not see any reason why Brad should bombard him with questions.

"If Jeff is too busy I'll take you myself," she told Beaudry.

"Oh, Jeff won't be too busy. He can take a half-day off," put in his father.

When Charlton left, Beulah followed him as far as the porch.

"Do you think Mr. Street is a horse-thief that you ask him so many questions?" she demanded indignantly.

He looked straight at her. "I don't know what he is, Beulah, but I'm going to find out."

"Isn't it possible that he is what he says he is?"

"Sure it's possible, but I don't believe it."

"Of course, I know you like to think the worst of a man, but when you meet him in my house I'll thank you to treat him properly. I vouch for him."

"You never met him before this afternoon."

"That's *my* business. It ought to be enough for you that he is my guest."

Charlton filled in the ellipsis. "If it isn't I can stay away, can't I? Well, I'm not going to quarrel with you, Beulah. Good-night."

As soon as he was out of sight of the ranch, Charlton turned the head of his horse, not toward his own place, but toward that of Jess Tighe.

Dr. Spindler drove up while Beulah was still on the porch. He examined the bruised ankle, dressed it, and pronounced that all it needed was a rest. No bones were broken, but the ligaments were strained. For several days she must give up riding and walking.

The ankle pained a good deal during the night, so that its owner slept intermittently. By morning she was no longer suffering, but was far too restless to stay in the house.

"I'm going to drive Mr. Street over to the Tighe place in the buggy," she announced at breakfast.

Her brothers exchanged glances.

"Think you'd better go so far with your bad ankle, honey?" Hal Rutherford, senior, asked.

"It doesn't make any difference, dad, so long as I don't put my weight on it."

She had her way, as she usually did. One of the boys hitched up and brought the team to the front of the house. Beaudry took the seat beside Beulah.

The girl gathered up the reins, nodded good-bye to her father, and drove off.

It was such a day as comes not more than a dozen times a season even in New Mexico. The pure light from the blue sky and the pine-combed air from the hills were like wine to their young blood. Once when the road climbed a hilltop the long saw-toothed range lifted before them, but mostly they could not see beyond the bastioned ramparts that hemmed in the park or the nearer wooded gulches that ran down from them.

Beulah had brought her camera. They took pictures of each other. They gathered wild flowers. They talked as eagerly as children. Somehow the bars were down between them. The girl had lost the manner of sullen resentment that had impressed him yesterday. She was gay and happy and vivid. Wild roses bloomed in her cheeks. For this young man belonged to the great world outside in which she was so interested. Other topics than horses and cattle and drinking-bouts were the themes of his talk. He had been to theaters and read books and visited large cities. His coming had enriched life for her.

The trail took them past a grove of young aspens which blocked the mouth of a small cañon by the thickness of the growth.

"Do you see any way in?" Beulah asked her companion.

"No. The trees are like a wall. There is not an open foot by which one could enter."

"Isn't there?" She laughed. "There's a way in just the same. You see that big rock over to the left? A trail drops down into the aspens back of it. A man lives in the gulch, an ex-convict. His name is Dan Meldrum."

"I expect he isn't troubled much with visitors."

"No. He lives alone. I don't like him, I wish he would move away. He doesn't do the park any good."

A man was sitting on the porch of the Tighe place as they drove up. Beside him lay a pair of crutches.

"That is Jess," the girl told Beaudry. "Don't mind if he is gruff or bad-tempered. He is soured."

But evidently this was not the morning for Tighe to be gruff. He came to meet them on his crutches, a smile on his yellow, sapless face. That smile seemed to Roy more deadly than anger. It did not warm the cold, malignant eyes nor light the mordant face with pleasure. Only the lips and mouth responded mechanically to it.

"Glad to see you, Miss Beulah. Come in."

He opened the gate and they entered. Presently Beaudry, his blood beating fast, found himself shaking hands with Tighe. The man had an odd trick of looking at one always from partly hooded eyes and at an angle.

"Mr. Street is selling windmills," explained Miss Rutherford. "Brad Charlton said you were talking of buying one, so here is your chance."

"Yes, I been thinking of it." Tighe's voice was suave. "What is your proposition, Mr. Street?"

Roy talked the Dynamo Aermotor for fifteen minutes. There was something about the still look of this man that put him into a cold sweat.

It was all he could do to concentrate his attention on the patter of a salesman, but he would not let his mind wander from the single track upon which he was projecting it. He knew he was being watched closely. To make a mistake might be fatal.

"Sounds good. I'll look your literature over, Mr. Street. I suppose you'll be in the park a few days?"

"Yes."

"Then you can come and see me again. I can't come to you so easy, Mr.—er—"

"Street," suggested Beulah.

"That's right—Street. Well, you see I'm kinder tied down." He indicated his crutches with a little lift of one hand. "Maybe Miss Beulah will bring you again."

"Suits me fine if she will," Beaudry agreed promptly.

The half-hooded eyes of the cripple slid to the girl and

back again to Roy. He had a way of dry-washing the backs of his hands like Uriah Heep.

"Fine. You'll stay to dinner, now, of course. That's good. That's good. Young folks don't know how it pleasures an old man to meet up with them sometimes." His low voice was as smooth as oil.

Beaudry conceived a horror of the man. The veiled sneer behind the smile on the sapless face, the hooded hawk eyes, the almost servile deference, held a sinister threat that chilled the spine of his guest. The young man thought of him as of a repulsive spider spinning a web of trouble that radiated from this porch all over the Big Creek country.

"Been taking pictures of each other, I reckon. Fine. Fine. Now, I wonder, Miss Beulah, if you'd do an old man a favor. This porch is my home, as you might say, seeing as how I'm sorter held down here. I'd kinder like a picture of it to hang up, providing it ain't asking too much of you."

"Of course not. I'll take it now," answered the girl.

"That's right good of you. I'll jest sit here and be talking to Mr. Street, as you might say. Wouldn't that make a good picture—kinder liven up the porch if we're on it?"

Roy felt a sudden impulse to protest, but he dared not yield to it. What was it this man wanted of the picture? Why had he baited a trap to get a picture of him without Beulah Rutherford knowing that he particularly wanted it? While the girl took the photograph, his mind was racing for Tighe's reason.

"I'll send you a copy as soon as I print it, Mr. Tighe,"

promised Beulah.

"I'll sure set a heap of store by it, Miss Beulah. . . . If you don't mind helping me set the table, we'll leave Mr. Street this old newspaper for a few minutes whilst we fix up a snack. You'll excuse us, Mr. Street? That's good."

Beulah went into the house the same gay and light-hearted comrade of Beaudry that she had been all morning. When he was called in to dinner, he saw at once that Tighe had laid his spell upon her. She was again the sullen, resentful girl of yesterday. Suspicion filmed her eyes. The eager light of faith in him that had quickened them while she listened for his answers to her naïve questions about the great world was blotted out completely.

She sat through dinner in cold silence. Tighe kept the ball of conversation rolling and Beaudry tried to play up to him. They talked of stock, crops, and politics. Occasionally the host diverted the talk to outside topics. He asked the young man politely how he liked the park, whether he intended to stay long, how long he had lived in New Mexico, and other casual questions.

Roy was glad when dinner was over. He drew a long breath of relief when they had turned their backs upon the ranch. But his spirits did not register normal even in the spring sunshine of the hills. For the dark eyes that met his were clouded with doubt and resentment.

CHAPTER 8

BEULAH ASKS QUESTIONS

A slim, wiry youth in high-heeled boots came out of the house with Brad Charlton just as the buggy stopped at the porch of the horse ranch. He nodded to Beulah.

" 'Lo, sis."

"My brother Ned—Mr. Street." The girl introduced them a little sulkily.

Ned Rutherford offered Roy a coffee-brown hand and looked at him with frank curiosity. He had just been hearing a lot about this good-looking stranger who had dropped into the park.

"See Jess Tighe? What did he say about the windmill?" asked Charlton.

"Wanted to think it over," answered Beaudry.

Beulah had drawn her brother to one side, but as Roy talked with Charlton he heard what the other two said, though each spoke in a low voice.

"Where you going, Ned?" the sister asked.

"Oh, huntin' strays."

"Home to-night?"

"Reckon not."

"What deviltry are you and Brad up to now? This will be the third night you've been away—and before that it was Jeff."

"S-sh!" Ned flashed a warning look in the direction of her guest.

But Beulah was angry. Tighe had warned her to be careful what she told Street. She distrusted the cripple profoundly. Half the evil that went on in the park was plotted by him. There had been a lot of furtive whispering about the house for a week or more. Her instinct told her that there was in the air some discreditable secret. More than once she had wondered whether her people had been the express company robbers for whom a reward was out. She tried to dismiss the suspicion from her mind, for the fear of it was like a leaden weight at her heart. But many little things contributed to the dread. Rutherford had sent her just at that time to spend the week at Battle Butte. Had it been to get her out of the way? She remembered that her father had made to her no explanation of that scene in which she and Dave Dingwell had played the leading parts. There had been many journeyings back and forth on the part of the boys and Charlton and her uncle, Buck Rutherford. They had a way of getting off into a corner of the corral and talking low for hours at a time. And now Street had come into the tangle. Were they watching him for fear he might be a detective?

Her resentment against him and them boiled over into swift wrath. "You're a fine lot—all of you. I'd like to wash my hands clean of the whole outfit." She turned on her heel and strode limping to the house.

Ned laughed as he swung to the back of one of the two broncos waiting with drooped heads before the porch. He admired this frank, forthright sister who blazed so handsomely into rage. He would have fought for her, even though he pretended to make a joke of her.

"Boots sure goes some. You see what you may be letting yourself in for, Brad," he scoffed good-naturedly.

Charlton answered with cool aplomb. "Don't you worry about me, Ned. I travel at a good lick myself. She'll break to double harness fine."

Without touching the stirrup this knight of the *chaparreras* flung himself into the saddle, the rowels of his spurs whirring as he vaulted. It was a spectacular but perfect mount. The horse was off instantly at a canter.

Roy could not deny the fellow admiration, even though he despised him for what he had just said. It was impossible for him to be contemptuous of Charlton. The man was too virile, too game for that. In the telling Western phrase, he would go through. Whatever he did was done competently.

Yet there was something detestable in the way he had referred to Beulah Rutherford. In the first place, Roy believed it to be a pure assumption that he was going to marry her. Then, too, he had spoken of this high-spirited girl as if she were a colt to be broken and he the man to wield the whip. Her rebellion against fate meant nothing more to him than a tantrum to be curbed. He did not in the least divine the spiritual unrest back of her explosion.

Beaudry shrugged his shoulders. He was lucky for once. It had been the place of Ned Rutherford to rebuke Charlton for his slighting remark. A stranger had not the least right to interfere while the brother of the girl was present. Roy did not pursue the point any further. He did not want to debate with himself whether he had the pluck to throw down the gauntlet to this fighting *vaquero* if the call had come to him.

As he walked into the house and up to his room, his

mind was busy with another problem. Where had Ned Rutherford been for three nights and his brother Jeff before that? Why had Beulah flared into unexpected anger? He, too, had glimpsed furtive whisperings. Even a fool would have understood that he was not a welcome guest at the horse ranch, and that his presence was tolerated only because here the boys could keep an eye on him. He was under surveillance. That was plain. He had started out for a little walk before breakfast and Jeff joined him from nowhere in particular to stroll along. What was it the Huerfano Park settlers were trying to hide from him? His mind jumped promptly to the answer. Dave Dingwell, of course.

Meanwhile Miss Rutherford lay weeping in the next room face down upon the bed. She rarely indulged in tears. It had not happened before since she was seventeen. But now she sobbed into a pillow, softly, so that nobody might hear. Why must she spend her life in such surroundings? If the books she read told the truth, the world was full of gentle, kindly people who lived within the law and respected each other's rights. Why was it in her horoscope to be an outcast? Why must she look at everybody with bitterness and push friendship from her lest it turn to poison at her touch? For one hour she had found joy in comradeship with this stranger. Then Tighe had whispered it that he was probably a spy. She had returned home only to have her doubts about her own family stirred to life again. Were there no good, honest folk in the world at all?

She washed her telltale eyes and ventured downstairs to look after supper. The Mexican cook was already peeling the potatoes. She gave him directions about the meal and went out to the garden to get some radishes and lettuce. On the way she had to pass the corral. Her brother Hal, Slim Sanders, and Cherokee Street were roping and branding some calves. The guest of the house had hung his coat and hat on a fence-post to keep them from getting soiled, but the hat had fallen into the dust.

Beulah picked up the hat and brushed it. As she dusted with her handkerchief the under side of the rim her eyes fell upon two initials stamped into the sweat pad. The letters were "R.B." The owner of the hat called himself Cherokee Street. Why, then, should he have these other initials printed on the pad? There could be only one answer to that question. He was passing under a name that was not his own.

If so why? Because he was a spy come to get evidence against her people for the express company.

The eyes of the girl blazed. The man had come to ruin her father, to send her brothers to prison, and he was accepting their hospitality while he moled for facts to convict them. To hear the shout of his gay laughter as a calf upset him in the dust was added fuel to the fire of her anger. If he had looked as villainous as Dave Meldrum, she could have stood it better, but any one would have sworn that he was a clean, decent young fellow just out of college.

She called to him. Roy glanced up and came across the corral. His sleeves were rolled to the elbows and the shirt open at the throat. Flowing muscles rippled under the white skin of his forearms as he vaulted the fence to stand beside her. He had the graceful poise of an athlete and the beautiful, trim figure of youth.

Yet he was a spy. Beulah hardened her heart.

"I found your hat in the dust, Mr. Street." She held it out to him upside down, the leather pad lifted by her finger so that the letters stood out.

The rigor of her eyes was a challenge. For a moment, before he caught sight of the initials, he was puzzled at her stiffness. Then his heart lost a beat and hammered wildly. His brain was in a fog and he could find no words of explanation.

"It is your hat, isn't it, Mr.—Street?"

"Yes." He took it from her, put it on, and gulped "Thanks."

She waited to give him a chance to justify himself, but he could find no answer to the charge that she had fixed upon him. Scornfully she turned from him and went to the house.

Miss Rutherford found her father reading a week-old newspaper.

"I've got fresher news than that for you, dad," she said. "I can tell you who this man that calls himself Cherokee Street isn't."

Rutherford looked up quickly. "You mean who he is, Boots."

"No, I mean who he isn't. His name isn't Cherokee Street at all."

"How do you know?"

"Because he is wearing a hat with the initials 'R.B.' stamped in it. I gave him a chance to explain and he only stammered and got white. He hadn't time to think up a lie that would fit."

"Dad burn it, Jess Tighe is right, then. The man is a spy." The ranchman lit a cigar and narrowed his eyes in thought.

"What is he spying here for?"

"I reckon he's a detective of the express company nosing around about that robbery. Some folks think it was pulled off by a bunch up in the hills somewhere."

"By the Rutherford gang?" she quoted.

He looked at her uneasily. The bitterness in her voice put him on the defensive. "Sho, Boots! That's just a way folks have of talking. We've got our enemies. Lots of people hate us because we won't let any one run over us."

She stood straight and slender before him, her eyes fixed in his. "Do they say we robbed the express company?"

"They don't say it out loud if they do—not where I can hear them," he answered grimly.

"Did we?" she flung at him.

His smile was forced. The question disturbed him. That had always been her way, even when she was a small child, to fling herself headlong at difficulties. She had never been the kind to be put off with anything less than the truth.

"I didn't. Did you?" he retorted.

"How about the boys—and Uncle Buck—and Brad Charlton?" she demanded.

"Better ask them if you want to know." With a flare of temper he contradicted himself. "No, you'd better mind your own business, girl. Forget your foolishness and 'tend to your knitting."

"I suppose it isn't my business if my kin go to the penitentiary for train robbery."

"They're not going any such place. If you want to know, I give you my word that none of us Rutherfords have got the gold stolen from the Western Express Company."

"And don't know where it is?"

"Haven't the least idea—not one of us."

She drew a deep breath of relief. More than once her father had kept from her secrets of the family activities, but he had never lied to her.

"Then it doesn't matter about this detective. He can find out nothing against us," she reflected aloud.

"I'm not so sure about that. We've had our troubles and we don't want them aired. There was that shooting scrape Hal got into down at Battle Butte, for instance. Get a little more evidence and the wrong kind of a jury would send him up for it. No, we'll keep an eye on Mr. Cherokee Street, or whatever his name is. Reckon I'll ride over and have a talk with Jess about it."

"Why not tell this man Street that he is not wanted and so be done with it?"

"Because we wouldn't be done with it. Another man would come in his place. We'll keep him here where we can do a little detective work on him, too."

"I don't like it. The thing is underhanded. I hate the fellow. It's not decent to sit at table with a man who is betraying our hospitality," she cried hotly.

"It won't be for long, honey. Just leave him to us. We'll hang up his pelt to dry before we're through with him."

"You don't mean—?"

"No, nothing like that. But he'll crawl out of the park like a whipped cur with its tail between its legs."

The cook stood in the doorway. "Miss Beulah, do you want that meat done in a pot roast?" he asked.

"Yes. I'll show you." She turned at the door. "By the way, dad, I took a snapshot of Mr. Tighe on his porch. I'll develop it to-night and you can take it to him in the morning."

"All right. Don't mention to anybody that matter we were discussing. Act like you've forgotten all about what you found out, Boots."

The girl nodded. "Yes."

CHAPTER 9

THE MAN ON THE BED

Beulah Rutherford found it impossible to resume a relation of friendliness toward her guest. By nature she was elemental and direct. A few months earlier she had become the teacher of the Big Creek school, but until that time life had never disciplined her to repress the impulses of her heart. As a child she had been a fierce, wild little creature full of savage affections and generosities. She still retained more feminine ferocity than social usage permits her sex. It was not in her to welcome an enemy with smiles while she hated him in her soul. The best she could do was to hold herself to a brusque civility whenever she met Beaudry.

As for that young man, he was in a most unhappy frame of mind. He writhed at the false position in which he found himself. It was bad enough to forfeit the good opinion of this primitive young hill beauty, but it was worse to know that in a measure he deserved it. He saw, too, that serious consequences were likely to follow her discovery, and he waited with nerves on the jump for the explosion.

None came. When he dragged himself to dinner, Beulah was stiff as a ramrod, but he could note no difference in the manner of the rest. Was it possible she had not told her father? He did not think this likely, and his heart was in panic all through the meal.

Though he went to his room early, he spent a sleepless night full of apprehension. What were the Rutherfords waiting for? He was convinced that something sinister lay behind their silence.

After breakfast the ranchman rode away. Jeff and Slim Sanders jogged off on their cowponies to mend a broken bit of fence. Hal sat on the porch replacing with rivets the torn strap of a stirrup.

Beaudry could stand it no longer. He found his hostess digging around the roots of some rosebushes in her small garden. Curtly she declined his offer to take the spade. For a minute he watched her uneasily before he blurted out his intention of going.

"I'll move up to the other end of the park and talk windmill to the ranchers there, Miss Rutherford. You've been awfully good to me, but I won't impose myself on your hospitality any longer," he said.

He had dreaded to make the announcement for fear of precipitating a crisis, but the young woman made no protest. Without a word of comment she walked beside him to the house.

"Hal, will you get Mr. Street's horse?" she asked her brother. "He is leaving this morning."

Young Rutherford's eyes narrowed. It was plain that he had been caught by surprise and did not know what to do.

"Where you going?" he asked.

"What do you care where he is going? Get the horse—or I will," she ordered imperiously.

"I'm going to board at one of the ranches farther up the park," explained Roy.

"Better wait till dad comes home," suggested Hal.

"No, I'll go now." Royal Beaudry spoke with the obstinacy of a timid man who was afraid to postpone the decision.

"No hurry, is there?" The black eyes of Rutherford fixed him steadily.

His sister broke in impatiently. "Can't he go when he wants to, Hal? Get Mr. Street's horse." She whirled on Beaudry scornfully. "That is what you call yourself, isn't it—Street?"

The unhappy youth murmured "Yes."

"Let him get his own horse if he wants to hit the trail in such a hurry," growled Hal sulkily.

Beulah walked straight to the stable. Awkwardly Beaudry followed her after a moment or two. The girl was leading his horse from the stall.

"I'll saddle him, Miss Rutherford," he demurred, the blanket in his hand.

She looked at him a moment, dropped the bridle, and turned stiffly away. He understood perfectly that she had been going to saddle the horse to justify the surface hospitality of the Rutherfords to a man they despised.

Hal was still on the porch when Roy rode up, but Beulah was nowhere in sight. The young hillman did not look up from the rivet he was driving. Beaudry swung to the ground and came forward.

"I'm leaving now. I should like to tell Miss Rutherford how much I'm in her debt for taking a stranger in so kindly," he faltered.

"I reckon you took her in just as much as she did you, Mr. Spy." Rutherford glowered at him menacingly. "I'd advise you to straddle that horse and git."

Roy controlled his agitation except for a slight trembling of the fingers that grasped the mane of his cowpony. "You've used a word that isn't fair. I didn't come here to harm any of your people. If I could explain to Miss Rutherford—"

She stood in the doorway, darkly contemptuous. Fire flashed in her eyes, but the voice of the girl was coldly insolent.

"It is not necessary," she informed him.

Her brother leaned forward a little. His crouched body looked like a coiled spring in its tenseness. "Explain yourself down that road, Mr. Street—*pronto,*" he advised.

Beaudry flashed a startled glance at him, swung to the saddle, and was away at a canter. The look in Rutherford's glittering eyes had sent a flare of fear over him. The impulse of it had lifted him to the back of the horse and out of the danger zone.

But already he was flogging himself with his own contempt. He had given way to panic before a girl who had been brought up to despise a quitter. She herself had nerves as steady as chilled steel. He had seen her clench her strong white little teeth without a murmur through a long afternoon of pain. Gameness was one of the fundamentals of her creed, and he had showed the white feather. It added to his punishment, too, that he worshiped pluck with all the fervor of one who knew he had none. Courage seemed to him the one virtue worth while; cowardice the unpardonable sin. He made no excuses for himself. From his father he inherited the fine tradition of standing up to punishment to a fighting finish. His mother, too, had been a thoroughbred. Yet he was a weakling. His heart pumped water instead of blood whenever the call to action came.

In dejection he rode up the valley, following the same hilly trail he had taken two days before with Miss Rutherford. It took him past the aspen grove at the mouth of the gulch which led to the Meldrum place. Beyond this a few hundred yards he left the main road and went through the chaparral toward a small ranch that nestled close to the timber. Beulah had told him that it belonged to an old German named Rothgerber who had lived there with his wife ever since she could remember.

Rothgerber was a little wrinkled old man with a strong South-German accent. After Beaudry had explained that he wanted board, the rancher called his wife out and the two jabbered away excitedly in their native tongue. The upshot of it was that they agreed to take the windmill agent if he would room in an old bunkhouse about two hundred yards from the main ranch building. This happened to suit Roy exactly and he closed the matter by paying for a week in advance.

The Rothgerbers were simple, unsuspecting people of a garrulous nature. It was easy for Beaudry to pump information from them while he ate supper. They had seen nothing of any stranger in the valley except himself, but they dropped casually the news that the Rutherfords had been going in and out of Chicito Cañon a good deal during the past few days.

"Chicito Cañon. That's a Mexican name, isn't it? Let's see. Just where is this gulch?" asked Beaudry.

The old German pointed out of the window. "There it iss, mein friend. You pass by on the road and there iss no way in—no arroyo, no gulch, no noddings but aspens. But there iss, shust the same, a trail. Through my pasture it leads."

"Anybody live up Chicito? I want everybody in the park to get a chance to buy a Dynamo Aermotor before I leave."

"A man named Meldrum. My advise iss—let him alone."

"Why?"

Rothgerber shook a pudgy forefinger in the air. "Mein friend—listen. You are a stranger in Huerfano Park. Gut. But do not ask questions about those who lif here. Me, I am an honest man. I keep the law. Also I mind my own pusiness. So it iss with many. But there are others—mind, I gif them no names, but—" He shrugged his shoulders and threw out his hands, palm up. "Well, the less said the petter. If I keep my tongue still, I do not talk myself into trouble. Not so, Berta?"

The pippin-cheeked little woman nodded her head sagely.

In the course of the next few days Roy rode to and fro over the park trying to sell his windmill to the ranchers. He secured two orders and the tentative promise of others. But he gained no clue as to the place where Dingwell was hidden. His intuition told him that the trail up Chicito Cañon would lead him to the captive cattleman. Twice he skirted the dark gash of the ravine at the back of the pasture, but each time his heart failed at the plunge into its unknown dangers. The first time he persuaded himself that he had better make the attempt at night, but when he stood on the brink in the darkness the gulf at his feet looked like a veritable descent into Avernus. If he should be caught down here, his fate would be sealed. What Meldrum and Tighe would do to a spy was not a matter of conjecture. The thought of it brought goose-quills to his flesh and tiny beads of perspiration to his forehead.

Still, the peril had to be faced. He decided to go up the cañon in the early morning before the travel of the day had begun. The night before he made the venture he prepared an alibi by telling Mrs. Rothgerber that he would not come to breakfast, as he wanted to get an early start for his canvassing. The little German woman bustled about and wrapped up for him a cold lunch to eat at his cabin in the morning. She liked this quiet, good-looking young man whose smile was warm for a woman almost old enough to be his grandmother. It was not often she met any one with the charming deference he showed her. Somehow he reminded her of her own Hans, who had died from the kick of a horse ten years since.

Roy slept in broken cat-naps full of fearful dreams, from which he woke in terror under the impression that he was struggling helplessly in the net of a great spider which had the cruel, bloodless face of Tighe. It was three o'clock when he rose and began to dress. He slipped out of the cabin into the wet pasture. His legs were sopping wet from the long grass through which he strode to the edge of the gulch. On a flat boulder he sat shivering in the darkness while he waited for the first gray streaks of light to sift into the dun sky.

In the dim dawn he stumbled uncertainly down the trail into the cañon, the bottom of which was still black as night from a heavy growth of young aspens that shut out the light. There was a fairly well-worn path leading up the gulch, so that he could grope his way forward slowly. His feet moved reluctantly. It seemed to him that his nerves, his brain, and even his muscles were in revolt against the moral compulsion that drove him on. He could feel his heart beating against his ribs. Every sound startled him. The still darkness took him by the throat. Doggedly he fought against the panic impulse to turn and fly.

If he quit now, he told himself, he could never hold his self-respect. He thought of all those who had come into his life in connection with the Big Creek country trouble. His father, his mother, Dave Dingwell, Pat Ryan, Jess Tighe, the whole Rutherford clan, including Beulah! One quality they all had in common, the gameness to see out to a finish anything they undertook. He could not go through life a confessed coward. The idea was intolerably humiliating.

Then, out of the past, came to him a snatch of nonsense verse:—

> "Li'l' ole hawss an' li'l' ole cow,
> Amblin' along by the ole haymow,
> Li'l' ole hawss took a bite an' a chew,
> 'Durned if I don't,' says the ole cow, too."

So vivid was his impression of the doggerel that for an instant he thought he heard the sing-song of his father's tuneless voice. In sharp, clean-cut pictures his memory reproduced the night John Beaudry had last chanted the lullaby and that other picture of the Homeric fight of one man against a dozen. The foolish words were a bracer to him. He set his teeth and ploughed forward, still with a quaking soul, but with a kind of despairing resolution.

After a mile of stiff going, the gulch opened to a little valley on the right-hand side. On the edge of a pine grove, hardly a stone's throw from where Roy stood, a Mexican *jacal* looked down into the cañon. The hut was a large one. It was built of upright poles daubed with clay. Sloping poles formed the roof, the chinks of which were waterproofed with grass. A wolf pelt, nailed to the wall, was hanging up to dry.

He knew that this was the home of Meldrum, the ex-convict.

Beaudry followed a bed of boulders that straggled toward the pine grove. It was light enough now, and he had to move with caution so as to take advantage of all the cover he could find. Once in the grove, he crawled from tree to tree. The distance from the nearest pine to the *jacal* was about thirty feet. A clump of *cholla* grew thick just outside the window. Roy crouched behind the trunk for several minutes before he could bring himself to take the chance of covering that last ten yards. But every minute it was getting lighter. Every minute increased the likelihood of detection. He crept fearfully to the hut, huddled behind the cactus, and looked into the window.

A heavy-set man, with the muscle-bound shoulders of an ape, was lighting a fire in the stove. At the table, his thumbs hitched in a sagging revolver belt, sat Ned Rutherford. The third person in the room lay stretched at supple ease on a bed to one of the posts of which his right leg was bound. He was reading a newspaper.

"Get a move on you, Meldrum," young Rutherford said jauntily, with an eye on his prisoner to see how he took it. "I've got inside information that I need some hot cakes, a few slices of bacon, and a cup of coffee. How about it, Dave? Won't you order breakfast, too?"

The man on the bed shook his head indifferently. "Me, I'm taking the fast cure. I been reading that we all eat too much, anyhow. What's the use of stuffing—gets yore system all clogged up. Now, take Edison—he don't eat but a handful of rice a day."

"That's one handful more than you been eating for the past three days. Better come through with what we want to know. This thing ain't going to get any better for you. A man has got to eat to live."

"I'm trying out another theory. Tell you-all about how it works in a week or so. I reckon after a time I'll get real hungry, but it don't seem like I could relish any chuck yet." The cattleman fell to perusing his paper once more.

Royal Beaudry had never met his father's friend, Dave Dingwell, but he needed no introduction to this brown-faced man who mocked his guard with such smiling hardihood. They were trying to starve the secret out of him. Already his cheek showed thin and gaunt, dark circles shadowed the eyes. The man, no doubt, was suffering greatly, yet his manner gave no sign of it. He might not be master of his fate; at least, he was very much the captain of his soul. Pat Ryan had described him in a sentence. "One hundred and ninety pounds of divil, and ivery ounce of ivery pound true gold." There could not be another man in the Big Creek country that this description fitted as well as it did this starving, jocund dare-devil on the bed.

The savory odor of bacon and of coffee came through the open window to Beaudry where he crouched in the chaparral. He heard Meldrum's brusque "Come and get it," and the sound of the two men drawing up their chairs to the table.

"What's the use of being obstinate, Dave?" presently asked Rutherford from amid a pleasant chink of tin cups, knives, and forks. "I'd a heap rather treat you like a white man. This 'Pache business doesn't make a hit with me. But I'm obeying orders. Anyhow, it's up to you. The chuck-wagon is ready for you whenever you say the word."

"I don't reckon I'll say it, Ned. Eating is just a habit. One man wants his eggs sunny side up; another is strong for them hard-boiled. But eggs is eggs. When Dan went visitin' at Santa Fé, he likely changed his diet. For two or three days he probably didn't like the grub, then—"

With a raucous curse the former convict swung round on him. A revolver seemed to jump to his hand, but before he could fire, young Rutherford was hanging to his wrist.

"Don't you, Dan. Don't you," warned Ned.

Slowly Meldrum's eyes lost their savage glare. "One o' these days I'll pump lead into him unless he clamps that mouth of his'n. I won't stand for it." His voice trailed into a string of oaths.

Apparently his host's fury at this reference to his convict days did not disturb in the least the man on the bed. His good-natured drawl grew slightly more pronounced. "Wall yore eyes and wave yore tail all you've a mind to, Dan. I was certainly some indiscreet reminding you of those days when you was a guest of the Government."

"That's enough," growled Meldrum, slamming his big fist down on the table so that the tinware jumped.

"Sure it's enough. Too much. Howcome I to be so forgetful? If I'd wore a uniform two years for rustling other folks' calves, I reckon I wouldn't thank a guy—"

But Meldrum had heard all he could stand. He had to do murder or get out. He slammed the coffee-pot down on the floor and bolted out of the open door. His arms whirled in violent gestures as he strode away. An unbroken stream of profanity floated back to mark his anabasis.

Meldrum did not once look round as he went on his explosive way to the gulch, but Roy Beaudry crouched lower behind the cactus until the man had disappeared.

Then he crawled back to the grove, slipped through it, and crept to the shelter of the boulder bed.

It would not do for him to return down the cañon during daylight, for fear he might meet one of the Rutherfords coming to relieve Ned. He passed from one boulder to another, always working up toward the wall of the gulch. Behind a big piece of sandstone shaped like a flatiron he lay down and waited for the hours to pass.

It was twilight when he stole down to the trail and began his return journey.

CHAPTER 10

DAVE TAKES A RIDE

Dave Dingwell had sauntered carelessly out of the Legal Tender on the night of his disappearance. He was apparently at perfect ease with a friendly world. But if any one had happened to follow him out of the saloon, he would have seen an odd change in the ranchman. He slid swiftly along the wall of the building until he had melted into the shadows of darkness. His eyes searched the neighborhood for lurking figures while he crouched behind the trunk of a cottonwood. Every nerve of the man was alert, every muscle ready for action. One brown hand lingered affectionately close to the butt of his revolver.

He had come out of the front door of the gambling-house because he knew the Rutherfords would expect him, in the exercise of ordinary common sense, to leave by the rear exit. That he would be watched was certain.

Therefore, he had done the unexpected and walked boldly out through the swinging doors.

As his eyes became accustomed to the darkness, he made out a horse in the clump of trees about twenty yards to the left. Whether it was Teddy he could not be sure, but there was no time to lose. Already a signal whistle had shrilled out from the other side of the street. Dave knew this was to warn the guards at the rear of the Legal Tender that their prey was in the open.

He made a dash for the tree clump, but almost as he reached it, he swung to the left and circled the small grove so as to enter it from the other side. As he expected, a man whirled to meet him. The unforeseen tactics of Dingwell had interfered with the ambush.

Dave catapulted into him head first and the two went down together. Before Dingwell could grip the throat of the man beneath him, a second body hurled itself through space at the cattleman. The attacked man flattened under the weight crushing him, but his right arm swept around and embraced the neck of his second assailant. He flexed his powerful forearm so as to crush as in a vice the throat of his foe between it and the hard biceps. The breath of the first man had for the moment been knocked out of him and he was temporarily not in the fight. The ranchman gave his full attention to the other.

The fellow struggled savagely. He had a gun in his right hand, but the fingers of Dave's left had closed upon the wrist above. Stertorous breathing gave testimony that the gunman was in trouble. In spite of his efforts to break the hold that kept his head in chancery, the muscles of the arm tightened round his neck like steel ropes drawn taut. He groaned, sighed in a ragged expulsion of breath, and suddenly collapsed.

Before he relaxed his muscles, Dingwell made sure that the surrender was a genuine one. His left hand slid down and removed the revolver from the nerveless fingers. The barrel of it was jammed against the head of the man above him while the rancher freed himself from the weight of the body. Slowly the cattleman got to his feet.

Vaguely he had been aware already that men were running toward the tree clump. Now he heard the padding of their feet close at hand. He ran to the horse and flung himself into the saddle, but before the animal had moved two steps some one had it by the bridle. Another man caught Dingwell by the arm and dragged him from the saddle. Before Dave could scramble to his feet again, something heavy fell upon his head and shook him to the heels. A thousand lights flashed in zigzags before his eyes. He sank back into unconsciousness.

The cowman returned to a world of darkness out of which voices came as from a distance hazily. A groan prefaced his arrival.

"Dave's waking up," one of the far voices said.

"Sure. When you tap his haid with a six-gun, you're liable to need repairs on the gun," a second answered.

The next words came to Dingwell more distinctly. He recognized the speaker as Hal Rutherford of the horse ranch.

"Too bad the boy had to hand you that crack, Dave. You're such a bear for fighting a man can't take any chances. Glad he didn't bust your haid wide open."

"Sure he didn't?" asked the injured man. "I feel like I got to hold it on tight so as to keep the blamed thing from flying into fifty pieces."

"Sorry. We'll take you to a doc and have it fixed up. Then we'll all go have a drink. That'll fix you."

"Business first," cut in Buck Rutherford.

"That's right, Dave," agreed the owner of the horse ranch. "How about that gunnysack? Where did you hide it?"

Dingwell played for time. He had not the least intention of telling, but if he held the enemy in parley some of his friends might pass that way.

"What gunnysack, Hal? Jee-rusalem, how my head aches!" He held his hands to his temples and groaned again.

"Your head will mend—if we don't have to give it another crack," Buck told him grimly. "Get busy, Dave. We want that gold—*pronto.* Where did you put it?"

"Where *did* I put it? That willing lad of yours has plumb knocked the answer out of my noodle. Maybe you're thinking of some one else, Buck." Dingwell looked up at him with an innocent, bland smile.

"Come through," ordered Buck with an oath.

The cattleman treated them to another dismal groan. "Gee! I feel like the day after Christmas. Was it a cannon the kid hit me with?"

Meldrum pushed his ugly phiz to the front. "Don't monkey away any time, boys. String him to one of these cottonwoods till he spits out what we want."

"Was it while you was visiting up at Santa Fé you

learnt that habit of seeing yore neighbors hanged, Dan?" drawled Dingwell in a voice of gentle irony.

Furious at this cool reference to his penitentiary days, Meldrum kicked their captive in the ribs. Hal Rutherford, his eyes blazing, caught the former convict by the throat.

"Do that again and I'll hang yore hide up to dry." He shook Meldrum as if he were a child, then flung the gasping man away. "I'll show you who's boss of this rodeo, by gum!"

Meldrum had several notches on his gun. He was, too, a rough-and-tumble fighter with his hands. But Hal Rutherford was one man he knew better than to tackle. He fell back, growling threats in his throat.

Meanwhile Dave was making discoveries. One was that the first two men who had attacked him were the gamblers he had driven from the Legal Tender earlier in the evening. The next was that Buck Rutherford was sending the professional tinhorns about their business.

"Git!" ordered the big rancher. "And keep gitting till you've crossed the border. Don't look back any. Jest burn the wind. *Adios*."

"They meant to gun you, Dave," guessed the owner of the horse ranch. "I reckon they daren't shoot with me loafing there across the road. You kinder disarranged their plans some more by dropping in at their back door. Looks like you'd 'a' rumpled up their hair a few if you hadn't been in such a hurry to make a get-away. Which brings us back to the previous question. The unanimous sense of the meeting is that you come through with some information, Dave. Where is that gunnysack?"

Dave, still sitting on the ground, leaned his back against a tree and grinned amiably at his questioner. "Sounds like you-all been to school to a parrot. You must 'a' quituated after you learned one sentence."

"We're waiting for an answer, Dave."

The cool, steady eyes of Dingwell met the imperious ones of the other man in a long even gaze. "Nothing doing, Hal."

"Even split, Dave. Fifty-fifty."

The sitting man shook his head. "I'll split the reward with you when I get it. The sack goes back to the express company."

"We'll see about that." Rutherford turned to his son and gave brisk orders. "Bring up the horses. We'll get out of here. You ride with me, Jeff. We'll take care of Dingwell. The rest of you scatter. We're going back to the park."

The Rutherfords and their captive followed no main road, but cut across country in a direction where they would be less likely to meet travelers. It was a land of mesquite and prickly pear. The sting of the cactus bit home in the darkness as its claws clutched at the riders winding their slow way through the chaparral.

Gray day was dawning when they crossed the Creosote Flats and were seen by a sheepherder at a distance. The sun was high in the heavens before they reached the defile which served as a getaway between the foothills and the range beyond. It had passed the meridian by the time they were among the summits where they could look back upon rounded hills numberless as the billows of a sea. Deeper and always deeper they plunged into the maze of cañons which gashed into the saddles between the peaks. Blue-tinted dusk was enveloping the hills as they dropped down through a wooded ravine into Huerfano Park.

"Home soon," Dave suggested cheerfully to his captors. "I sure am hungry enough to eat a government mailsack. A flank steak would make a big hit with me."

Jeff looked at him in the dour, black Rutherford way. "This is no picnic, you'll find."

"Not to you, but it's a great vacation for me. I feel a hundred per cent better since I got up into all this ozone and scenery," Dingwell assured him hardily. "A man ought to take a trip like this every once in a while. It's great for what ails him."

Young Rutherford grunted sulkily. Their prisoner was the coolest customer he had ever met. The man was no fool. He must know he was in peril, but his debonair, smiling insouciance never left him for a moment. He was grit clear through.

CHAPTER 11

TIGHE WEAVES HIS WEB TIGHTER

The hooded eyes of Jess Tighe slanted across the table at his visitor. Not humor but mordant irony had given birth to the sardonic smile on his thin, bloodless lips.

"I reckon you'll be glad to know that you've been entertaining an angel unawares, Hal," he jeered. "I've been looking up your handsome young friend, and I can tell you what the 'R.B.' in his hat stands for in case you would be interested to know."

The owner of the horse ranch gave a little nod. "Unload your information, Jess."

Tighe leaned forward for emphasis and bared his teeth. If ever malevolent hate was written on a face it found expression on his now.

"'R. B.' stands for Royal Beaudry."

Rutherford flashed a question at him from startled eyes. He waited for the other man to continue.

"You remember the day we put John Beaudry out of business?" asked Tighe.

"Yes. Go on." Hal Rutherford was not proud of that episode. In the main he had fought fair, even though he had been outside the law. But on the day he had avenged the death of his brother Anson, the feud between him and the sheriff had degenerated to murder. A hundred times since he had wished that he had gone to meet the officer alone.

"He had his kid with him. Afterward they shipped him out of the country to an aunt in Denver. He went to school there. Well, I've had a little sleuthing done."

"And you've found out—?"

"What I've told you."

"How?"

"He said his name was Cherokee Street, but Jeff told me he didn't act like he believed himself. When yore girl remembered there was a street of that name in Denver, Mr. Cherokee Street was plumb rattled. He seen he'd made a break. Well, you saw that snapshot Beulah took of him and me on the porch. I sent it to a detective agency in Denver with orders to find out the name of the man that photo fitted. My idea was for the manager to send a man to the teachers of the high schools, beginning with the school nearest Cherokee Street. He done it. The third schoolmarm took one look at the picture and said the young fellow was Royal Beaudry. She had taught him German two years. That's howcome I to know what that 'R.B.' in the hat stands for."

"Perhaps it is some other Beaudry."

"Take another guess," retorted the cripple scornfully. "Right off when I clapped eyes on him, I knew he reminded me of somebody. I know now who it was."

"But what's he doing up here?" asked the big man.

The hawk eyes of Tighe glittered. "What do you reckon the son of John Beaudry would be doing here?" He answered his own question with bitter animosity. "He's gathering evidence to send Hal Rutherford and Jess Tighe to the penitentiary. That's what he's doing."

Rutherford nodded. "Sure. What else would he be doing if he is a chip off the old block? That's where his father's son ought to put us if he can."

Tighe beat his fist on the table, his face a map of appalling fury and hate. "Let him go to it, then. I've been a cripple seventeen years because Beaudry shot me up. By God! I'll gun his son inside of twenty-four hours. I'll stomp him off'n the map like he was a rattlesnake."

"No," vetoed Rutherford curtly.

"What! What's that you say?" snarled the other.

"I say he'll get a run for his money. If there's any killing to be done, it will be in fair fight."

"What's ailing you?" sneered Tighe. "Getting soft in your upper story? Mean to lie down and let that kid run you through to the pen like his father did Dan Meldrum?"

"Not in a thousand years," came back Rutherford. "If he wants war, he gets it. But I'll not stand for any killing from ambush, and no killing of any kind unless it has to be. Understand?"

"That sounds to me," purred the smaller man in the Western slang that phrased incredulity. Then, suddenly, he foamed at the mouth. "Keep out of this if you're squeamish. Let me play out the hand. I'll bump him off *pronto.*"

"No, Jess."

"What do you think I am?" screamed Tighe. "Seventeen years I've been hog-tied to this house because of Beaudry. Think I'm going to miss my chance now? If he was Moody and Sankey rolled into one, I'd go through with it. And what is he—a spy come up here to gather evidence against you and me! Didn't he creep into your house so as to sell you out when he got the goods? Hasn't he lied from start to finish?"

"Maybe so. But he has no proof against us yet. We'll kick him out of the park. I'm not going to have his blood on my conscience. That's flat, Jess."

The eyes in the bloodless face of the other man glittered, but he put a curb on his passion. "What about me, Hal? I've waited half a lifetime and now my chance has come. Have you forgot who made me the misshaped thing I am? I haven't. I'll go through hell to fix Beaudry's cub the way he did me." His voice shook from the bitter intensity of his feeling.

Rutherford paced up and down the room in a stress of

sentiency. "No, Jess. I know just how you feel, but I'm going to give this kid his chance. We gunned Beaudry because he wouldn't let us alone. Either he or a lot of us had to go. But I'll say this. I never was satisfied with the way we did it. When Jack Beaudry shot you up, he was fighting for his life. We attacked him. You got no right to hold it against his son."

"I don't ask you to come in. I'll fix his clock all right."

"Nothing doing. I won't have it." Rutherford, by a stroke of strategy, carried the war into the country of the other. "I gave way to you about Dingwell, though I hated to try that Indian stuff on him. He's a white man. I've always liked him. It's a rotten business."

"What else can you do? We daren't turn him loose. You don't want to gun him. There is nothing left but to tighten the thumbscrews."

"It won't do any good," protested the big man with a frown. "He's game. He'll go through. . . . And if it comes to a showdown, I won't have him starved to death."

Tighe looked at him through half-hooded, cruel eyes. "He'll weaken. Another day or two will do it. Don't worry about Dingwell."

"There's not a yellow streak in him. You haven't a chance to make him quit." Rutherford took another turn up and down the room diagonally. "I don't like this way of fighting. It's damnable, man! I won't have any harm come to Dave or to the kid either. I stand pat on that, Jess."

The man with the crutches swallowed hard. His Adam's apple moved up and down like an agitated thermometer. When he spoke it was in a smooth, oily voice of submission, but Rutherford noticed that the rapacious eyes were hooded.

"What you say goes, Hal. You're boss of this round-up. I was jest telling you how it looked to me."

"Sure. That's all right, Jess. But you want to remember that public sentiment is against us. We've pretty near gone our limit up here. If there was no other reason but that, it would be enough to make us let this young fellow alone. We can't afford a killing in the park now."

Tighe assented, almost with servility. But the cattleman carried away with him a conviction that the man had yielded too easily, that his restless brain would go on planning destruction for young Beaudry just the same.

He was on his way up Chicito Cañon and he stopped at Rothgerber's ranch to see Beaudry. The young man was not at home.

"He start early this morning to canfass for his vindmill," the old German explained.

After a moment's thought Rutherford left a message. "Tell him it isn't safe for him to stay in the park; that certain parties know who 'R.B.' is and will sure act on that information. Say I said for him to come and see me as soon as he gets back. Understand? Right away when he reaches here."

The owner of the horse ranch left his mount in the Rothgerber corral and passed through the pasture on foot to Chicito. Half an hour later he dropped into the *jacal* of Meldrum.

He found the indomitable Dingwell again quizzing Meldrum about his residence at Santa Fé during the days he wore a striped uniform. The former convict was grinding his teeth with fury.

"I reckon you won't meet many old friends when you go back this time, Dan. Maybe there will be one or two old-timers that will know you, but it won't be long before you make acquaintances," Dave consoled him.

"Shut up, or I'll pump lead into you," he warned hoarsely.

The cattleman on the bed shook his head. "You'd like to fill me full of buckshot, but it wouldn't do at all, Dan. I'm the goose that lays the golden eggs, in a way of speaking. Gun me, and it's good-bye to that twenty thousand in the gunnysack." He turned cheerfully to Rutherford, who was standing in the doorway. "Come right in, Hal. Glad to see you. Make yourself at home."

"He's deviling me all the time," Meldrum complained to the owner of the horse ranch. "I ain't a-going to stand it."

Rutherford looked at the prisoner, a lean, hard-bitten Westerner with muscles like steel ropes and eyes unblinking as a New Mexico sun. His engaging recklessness had long since won the liking of the leader of the Huerfano Park outlaws.

"Don't bank on that golden egg business, Dave," advised Rutherford. "If you tempt the boys enough, they're liable to forget it. You've been behaving mighty aggravating to Dan."

"Me!" Dave opened his eyes in surprise. "I was just asking him how he'd like to go back to Santa Fé after you-all turn me loose."

"We're not going to turn you loose till we reach an agreement. What's the use of being pigheaded? We're looking for that gold and we're going to find it mighty soon. Now be reasonable."

"How do you know you're going to find it?"

"Because we know you couldn't have taken it far. Here's the point. You had it when Fox made his getaway. Beulah was right behind you, so we know you didn't get a chance to bury it between there and town. We covered your tracks and you didn't leave the road in that half-mile. That brings you as far as Battle Butte. You had the gunnysack when you crossed the bridge. You didn't have it when Slim Sanders met you. So you must have got rid of it in that distance of less than a quarter of a mile. First off, I figured you dropped the sack in Hague's alfalfa field. But, we've tramped that all over. It's not there. Did you meet some one and give it to him? Or how did you get rid of it?"

"I ate it," grinned Dingwell confidentially.

"The boys are getting impatient, Dave. They don't like the way you butted in."

"That's all right. You're responsible for my safety, Hal. I'll let you do the worrying."

"Don't fool yourself. We can't keep you here forever. We can't let you go without an agreement. Figure out for yourself what's likely to happen?"

"Either my friends will rescue me, or else I'll escape."

"Forget it. Not a chance of either." Rutherford stopped, struck by an idea. "Ever hear of a young fellow called Cherokee Street?"

"No. Think not. Is he a breed?"

"White man." Rutherford took a chair close to Dingwell. He leaned forward and asked another question in a low voice. "Never happened to meet the son of John Beaudry, did you?"

Dingwell looked at him steadily out of narrowed eyes. "I don't get you, Hal. What has he got to do with it?"

"Thought maybe you could tell me that. He's in the park now."

"In the park?"

"Yes—and Jess Tighe knows it."

"What's he doing here?"

But even as he asked the other man, Dingwell guessed the answer. Not an hour before he had caught a glimpse of a white, strained face at the window. He knew now whose face it was.

"He's spying on us and sleuthing for evidence to send us to the pen. Think he'd be a good risk for an insurance company?"

Dave thought fast. "I don't reckon you're right. I put the kid through law school. My friends have likely sent him up here to look for me."

Rutherford scoffed. "Nothing to that. How could they know you are here? We didn't advertise it."

"No-o, but—" Dingwell surrendered the point reluctantly. He flashed a question at Rutherford. "Tighe will murder him. That's sure. You going to let him?"

"Not if I can help it. I'm going to send young Beaudry out of the park."

"Fine. Don't lose any time about it, Hal."

The Huerfano Park rancher made one more attempt to shake his prisoner. His dark eyes looked straight into those of Dingwell.

"Old-timer, what about you? I ain't enjoying this any

more than you are. But it's clear out of my hands."

"Then why worry?" asked Dingwell, a little grin on his drawn face.

"Hell! What's the use of asking that? I'm no Injun devil," barked Rutherford irritably.

"Turn me loose and I'll forget all I've seen. I won't give you the loot, but I'll not be a witness against you."

The Huerfano Park ranchman shook his head. "No, we want that gold, Dave. You butted into our game and we won't stand for that."

"I reckon we can't make a deal, Hal."

The haggard eyes of the starving man were hard as tungsten-washed steel. They did not yield a jot.

A troubled frown dragged together the shaggy eyebrows of Rutherford as he snapped out his ultimatum.

"I like you, Dave. Always have. But you're in one hell of a hole. Don't feed yourself any fairy tales. Your number is chalked up, my friend. Unless you come through with what we want, you'll never leave here alive. I can't save you. There's only one man can—and that is your friend David Dingwell."

The other man did not bat an eyelid. "Trying to pass the buck, Hal? You can't get away with it—not for a minute." A gay little smile of derision touched his face. "I'm in your hands completely. I'll not tell you a damn thing. What are you going to do about it? No, don't tell me that Meldrum and Tighe will do what has to be done. You're the high mogul here. If they kill me, Hal Rutherford will be my murderer. Don't forget that for a second."

Rutherford carried home with him a heavy heart. He

could see no way out of the difficulty. He knew that neither Meldrum nor Tighe would consent to let Dingwell go unless an agreement was first reached. There was, too, the other tangle involving young Beaudry. Perhaps he also would be obstinate and refuse to follow the reasonable course.

Beulah met him on the road. Before they had ridden a hundred yards, her instinct told her that he was troubled.

"What is it, dad?" she asked.

He compromised with himself and told her part of what was worrying him. "It's about your friend Street. Jess had him looked up in Denver. The fellow turns out to be a Royal Beaudry. You've heard of a sheriff of that name who used to live in this country? . . . Well, this is his son."

"What's he doing here?"

"Trying to get us into trouble, I reckon. But that ain't the point. I'm not worrying about what he can find out. Fact is that Tighe is revengeful. This boy's father crippled him. He wants to get even on the young fellow. Unless Beaudry leaves the park at once, he'll never go. I left word at Rothgerber's for him to come down and see me soon as he gets home."

"Will he come?" she asked anxiously.

"I don't know. If not I'll go up and fetch him. I don't trust Jess a bit. He'll strike soon and hard."

"Don't let him, dad," the girl implored.

The distressed eyes of the father rested on her. "You like this young fellow, honey?" he asked.

She flamed. "I hate him. He abused our hospitality. He lied to us and spied on us. I wouldn't breathe the same air he does if I could help it. But we can't let him be killed in cold blood."

"That's right, Boots. Well, he'll come down to-day and I'll pack him back to Battle Butte. Then we'll be shet of him."

Beulah passed the hours in a fever of impatience. She could not keep her mind on the children she was teaching. She knew Tighe. The decision of her father to send Beaudry away would spur the cripple to swift activity. Up at Rothgerber's Jess could corner the man and work his vengeance unhampered. Why did not the spy come down to the horse ranch? Was it possible that his pride would make him neglect the warning her father had left? Perhaps he would think it only a trap to catch him.

Supper followed dinner, and still Beaudry had not arrived. From the porch Beulah peered up the road into the gathering darkness. Her father had been called away. Her brothers were not at home. The girl could stand it no longer. She went to the stable and saddled Blacky.

Five minutes later she was flying up the road that led to the Rothgerber place.

CHAPTER 12

STARK FEAR

When Beaudry climbed the cañon wall to the Rothgerber pasture he breathed a deep sigh of relief. For many hours he had been under a heavy strain, nerves taut as fiddle-strings. Fifty times his heart had jumped with terror. But he had done the thing he had set out to do.

He had stiffened his flaccid will and spurred his trembling body forward. If he had been unable to control his fear, at least he had not let it master him. He had found out for Ryan where Dingwell was held prisoner. It had been his intention to leave the park as soon as he knew this, report the facts to the friends of Dave, and let them devise a way of escape. He had done his full share. But he could not follow this course now.

The need of the cattleman was urgent. Somehow it must be met at once. Yet what could he do against two armed men who would not hesitate to shoot him down if necessary? There must be some way of saving Dingwell if he could only find it.

In spite of his anxiety, a fine spiritual exaltation flooded him. So far he had stood the acid test, had come through without dishonor. He might be a coward; at least, he was not a quitter. Plenty of men would have done his day's work without a tremor. What brought comfort to Roy's soul was that he had been able to do it at all.

Mrs. Rothgerber greeted him with exclamations of delight. The message of Rutherford had frightened her even though she did not entirely understand it.

"Hermann iss out looking for you. Mr. Rutherford—the one that owns the horse ranch—he wass here and left a message for you."

"A message for me! What was it?"

With many an "Ach!" she managed to tell him.

The face of her boarder went white. Since Rutherford was warning him against Tighe, the danger must be imminent. Should he go down to the horse ranch now? Or had he better wait until it was quite dark? While he was still debating this with himself, the old German came into the house.

"Home, eh? Gut, gut! They are already yet watching the road."

Roy's throat choked. "Who?"

This question Rothgerber could not answer. In the dusk he had not recognized the men he had seen. Moreover, they had ridden into the brush to escape observation. Both of them had been armed with rifles.

The old woman started to light a lamp, but Roy stopped her. "Let's eat in the dark," he proposed. "Then I'll slip out to the bunkhouse and you can have your light."

His voice shook. When he tried to eat, his fingers could scarcely hold a knife and fork. Supper was for him a sham. A steel band seemed to grip his throat and make the swallowing of food impossible. He was as unnerved as a condemned criminal waiting for the noose.

After drinking a cup of coffee, he pushed back his chair and rose.

"Petter stay with us," urged the old German. He did not know why this young man was in danger, but he read in the face the stark fear of a soul in travail.

"No. I'll saddle and go down to see Rutherford. Goodnight."

Roy went out of the back door and crept along the shadows of the hill. Beneath his foot a dry twig snapped. It was enough. He fled panic-stricken, pursued by all the demons of hell his fears could evoke. A deadly, unnerving terror clutched at his throat. The pounding blood seemed ready to burst the veins at his temples.

The bunkhouse loomed before him in the darkness. As he plunged at the door a shot rang out. A bolt of fire burned into his shoulder. He flung the door open, slammed it shut behind him, locked and bolted it almost with one motion. For a moment he leaned half swooning against the jamb, sick through and through at the peril he had just escaped.

But had he escaped it? Would they not break in on him and drag him out to death? The acuteness of his fright drove away the faintness. He dragged the bed from its place and pushed it against the door. Upon it he piled the table, the washstand, the chairs. Feverishly he worked to barricade the entrance against his enemies.

When he had finished, his heart was beating against his ribs like that of a wild rabbit in the hands of a boy. He looked around for the safest place to hide. From the floor he stripped a Navajo rug and pulled up the trapdoor that led to a small cellar stairway. Down into this cave he went, letting the door fall shut after him.

In that dark blackness he waited, a crumpled, trembling wretch, for whatever fate might have in store for him.

How long he crouched there Beaudry never knew. At last reason asserted itself and fought back the panic. To stay where he was would be to invite destruction. His attackers would come to the window. The barricaded door, the displaced rug, the trapdoor, would advertise his terror. The outlaws would break in and make an end of him.

Roy could hardly drag his feet up the stairs, so near was he to physical collapse. He listened. No sound reached him. Slowly he pushed up the trapdoor. Nobody was in the room. He crept up, lowered the door, and replaced the carpet. With his eyes on the window he put back the furniture where it belonged. Then, revolver in hand, he sat in one corner of the room and tried to decide what he must do.

Down in the cellar he had been vaguely aware of a dull pain in his shoulder and a wet, soggy shirt above the place. But the tenseness of his anxiety had pushed this into the background of his thoughts. Now again the throbbing ache intruded itself. The fingers of his left hand searched under his waistcoat, explored a spot that was tender and soppy, and came forth moist.

He knew he had been shot, but this gave him very little concern. He had no time to worry about his actual ills, since his whole mind was given to the fear of those that were impending.

Upon the window there came a faint tapping. The hand with the revolver jerked up automatically. Every muscle of Beaudry's body grew rigid. His senses were keyed to a tense alertness. He moistened his lips with his tongue as he crouched in readiness for the attack about to break.

Again the tapping, and this time with it a quick, low, imperious call.

"Mr. Street. Are you there? Let me in!"

He knew that voice—would have known it among a thousand. In another moment he had raised the window softly and Beulah Rutherford was climbing in.

She panted as if she had been running. "They're

watching the entrance to the arroyo. I came up through the cañon and across the pasture," she explained.

"Did they see you?"

"No. Think not. We must get out of here."

"How?"

"The same way I came."

"But—if they see us and shoot?"

The girl brushed his objection aside. "We can't help that. They know you're here, don't they?"

"Yes."

"Then they'll rush the house. Come."

Still he hesitated. At least they had the shelter of the house. Outside, if they should be discovered, they would be at the mercy of his foes.

"What are you waiting for?" she asked sharply, and she moved toward the window.

But though he recoiled from going to meet the danger, he could not let a girl lead the way. Beaudry dropped to the ground outside and stood ready to lend her a hand. She did not need one. With a twist of her supple body Beulah came through the opening and landed lightly beside him.

They crept back to the shadows of the hill and skirted its edge. Slowly they worked their way from the bunkhouse, making the most of such cover as the chaparral afforded. Farther up they crossed the road into the pasture and by way of it reached the orchard. Every inch of the distance Roy sweated fear.

She was leading, ostensibly because she knew the lay of the land better. Through the banked clouds the moon was struggling. Its light fell upon her lithe, slender figure, the beautifully poised head, the crown of soft black hair. She moved with the grace and the rhythm of a racing filly stepping from the paddock to the track.

Beaudry had noticed, even in his anxiety, that not once since the tapping on the window had her hand touched his or the sweep of her skirt brushed against his clothes. She would save him if she could, but with an open disdain that dared him to misunderstand.

They picked their course diagonally through the orchard toward the cañon. Suddenly Beulah stopped. Without turning, she swept her hand back and caught his. Slowly she drew him to the shadow of an apple tree. There, palm to palm, they crouched together.

Voices drifted to them.

"I'd swear I hit him," one said.

"Maybe you put him out of business. We got to find out," another answered.

"I'll crawl up to the window and take a look," responded the first.

The voices and the sound of the men's movements died. Beulah's hand dropped to her side.

"We're all right now," she said coldly.

They reached the gulch and slowly worked their way down its precipitous sides to the bottom.

The girl turned angrily on Roy. "Why didn't you come after father warned you?"

"I didn't get his warning till night. I was away."

"Then how did you get back up the arroyo when it was watched?"

"I—I wasn't out into the park," he told her.

"Oh!" Her scornful gypsy eyes passed over him and

wiped him from the map. She would not even comment on the obvious alternative.

"You think I've been up at Dan Meldrum's spying," he protested hotly.

"Haven't you?" she flung at him.

"Yes, if that's what you want to call it," came quickly his bitter answer. "The man who has been my best friend is lying up there a prisoner because he knows too much about the criminals of Huerfano Park. I heard Meldrum threaten to kill him unless he promised what was wanted of him. Why shouldn't I do my best to help the man who—"

Her voice, sharpened by apprehension, cut into his. "What man? Who are you talking about?"

"I'm talking about David Dingwell."

"What do you mean that he knows too much? Too much about what?" she demanded.

"About the express robbery."

"Do you mean to say that—that my people—?" She choked with anger, but back of her indignation was fear.

"I mean to say that one of your brothers was guarding Dingwell and that later your father went up to Meldrum's place. They are starving him to get something out of him. I serve warning on you that if they hurt my friend—"

"Starving him!" she broke out fiercely. "Do you dare say that my people—my father—would torture anybody? Is that what you mean, you lying spy?"

Her fury was a spur to him. "I don't care what words you use," he flung back wildly. "They have given him no food for three days. I didn't know such things were done nowadays. It's as bad as what the old Apaches did. It's devilish—"

He pulled himself up. What right had he to talk that way to the girl who had just saved his life? Her people might be law-breakers, but he felt that she was clean of any wrong-doing.

Her pride was shaken. A more immediate issue had driven it into the background.

"Why should they hurt him?" she asked. "If they had meant to do that—"

"Because he won't tell what he knows—where the gold is—won't promise to keep quiet about it afterward. What else can they do? They can't turn him loose as a witness against them."

"I don't believe it. I don't believe a word of it." Her voice broke. "I'm going up to see right away."

"You mean—to-night?"

"I mean now."

She turned up the gulch instead of down. Reluctantly he followed her.

CHAPTER 13

BEULAH INTERFERES

They felt their way up in the darkness. The path was rough and at first pitch-black. After a time they emerged from the aspens into more open travel. Here were occasional gleams of light, as if the moon stood tip-toe and peered down between the sheer walls of Chicito to the obscure depths below.

Beulah led. Mountain-born and bred, she was active as a bighorn. Her slenderness was deceptive. It concealed the pack of her long rippling muscles, the deep-breasted strength of her torso. One might have marched a long day's journey without finding a young woman more perfectly modeled for grace and for endurance.

"What are you going to try to do?" Beaudry asked of her timidly.

She turned on him with a burst of feminine ferocity. "Is that any of your business? I didn't ask you to come with me, did I? Go down to the horse ranch and ask dad to help you out of the park. Then, when you're safe with your friends, you can set the officers on him. Tell them he is a criminal—just as you told me."

Her biting tongue made him wince. "If I told you that I'm sorry. I had no right. You've saved my life. Do you think it likely I would betray your people after that?"

"How do I know what a spy would do? Thank God, I can't put myself in the place of such people," she answered disdainfully.

He smiled ruefully. She was unjust, of course. But that did not matter. Roy knew that she was wrought up by what he had told her. Pride and shame and hatred and distrust spoke in her sharp words. Was it not natural that a high-spirited girl should resent such a charge against her people and should flame out against the man who had wounded her? Even though she disapproved of what they had done, she would fly to their defense when attacked.

From the dark gash of the ravine they came at last to the opening where Meldrum lived.

The young woman turned to Beaudry. "Give me your revolver belt."

He hesitated. "What are you going to do?"

Plainly she would have liked to rebuff him, but just now he had the whip hand. Her sullen answer came slowly.

"I'm going to tell my brother that father needs him. When he has gone, I'll see what I can do."

"And what am I to do while you are inside?"

"Whatever you like." She held out her hand for his belt.

Not at all willingly he unbuckled it. "You'll be careful," he urged. "Meldrum is a bad man. Don't try any tricks with him."

"He knows better than to touch a hair of my head," she assured him with proud carelessness. Then, "Hide in those trees," she ordered.

Ned Rutherford answered her knock on the door of the *jacal.* At sight of her he exclaimed:—

"What are you doing here, Boots? At this time of night? Anything wrong?"

"Dad needs you, Ned. It seems there is trouble about that young man Street. Jess Tighe has sworn to kill him and dad won't have it. There's trouble in the air. You're to come straight home."

"Why didn't he send Jeff?"

"He needed him. You're to keep on down through the cañon to the mouth. Jess has the mouth of the arroyo guarded to head off Street."

"But—what's broke? Why should Tighe be so keen on bumping off this pink-ear when dad says no?"

"They've found out who he is. It seems Street is an alias. He is really Royal Beaudry, the son of the man who used to be sheriff of the county, the one who crippled Jess the day he was killed."

The slim youth in the high-heeled boots whistled. He understood now why Tighe dared to defy his father.

"All right, Boots. With you in a minute, soon as I get my hat and let Dan know."

"No. I'm to stay here till dad sends for me. He doesn't want me near the trouble."

"You mean you're to stay at Rothgerber's."

"No, here. Tighe may attack Rothgerber's any time to get this young Beaudry. I heard shooting as I came up."

"But—you can't stay here. What's dad thinking about?" he frowned.

"If you mean because of Mr. Dingwell, I know all about that."

"Who told you?" he demanded.

"Dad can't keep secrets from me. There's no use his trying."

"Hm! I notice he loaded us with a heap of instructions not to let you know anything. He'd better learn to padlock his own tongue."

"Isn't there a room where I can sleep here?" Beulah asked.

"There's a cot in the back room," he admitted sulkily. "But you can't—"

"That's another thing," she broke in. "Dad doesn't want Dan left alone with Mr. Dingwell."

"Who's that out there, Ned?" growled a heavy voice from inside.

Beulah followed her brother into the hut. Two men stared at her in amazement. One sat on the bed with a leg tied to the post. The other was at the table playing solitaire, a revolver lying beside the cards. The card-player was Meldrum. He jumped up with an oath.

"Goddlemighty! What's she doing here?" he demanded in his hoarse raucous bass.

"That's her business and mine," Rutherford answered haughtily.

"It's mine too, by God! My neck's in the noose, ain't it?" screamed the former convict. "Has everybody in the park got to know we're hiding Dingwell here? Better put it in the paper. Better—"

"Enough of that, Dan. Dad is running this show. Obey orders, and that lets you out," retorted the young man curtly. "You've met my sister, haven't you, Dave?"

The cattleman smiled at the girl. "Sure. We had a little ride together not long since. I owe you a new raincoat. Don't I, Miss Beulah?"

She blushed a little. "No, you don't, Mr. Dingwell. The mud came off after it dried."

"That's good." Dave turned to Rutherford. The little devils of mischief were in his eyes. "Chet Fox was with us, but he didn't stay—had an engagement, he said. He was in some hurry to keep it, too."

But though he chatted with them gayly, the ranchman's mind was subconsciously busy with the new factor that had entered into the problem of his captivity. Why had Rutherford allowed her to come? He could not understand that. Every added one who knew that he was here increased the danger to his abductors. He knew how fond the owner of the horse ranch was of this girl. It was odd that he had let her become involved in his lawless plans. Somehow that did not seem like Hal Rutherford. One point that stood out like the Map of Texas brand was the effect of her coming upon his chances. To secure their safety neither Tighe nor Meldrum would stick at murder. Ten minutes ago the prudent way out of the difficulty would have been for them to arrange his death by accident. Now this was no longer feasible. When the Rutherford girl had stepped into the conspiracy, it became one of finesse and not bloodshed. Was this the reason that her father had sent her—to stay the hands of his associates already reaching toward the prisoner? There was no question that Meldrum's finger had been itching on the trigger of his revolver for a week. One of the young Rutherfords had been beside him day and night to restrain the man.

Dave was due for another surprise when Ned presently departed after a whispered conference with Meldrum and left his sister in the hut. Evidently something important was taking place in another part of the park. Had it to do with young Beaudry?

From his reflections the cattleman came to an alert attention. Miss Rutherford was giving Meldrum instructions to arrange her bed in the back room.

The convict hesitated. "I can't leave him here alone with you," he remonstrated surlily.

"Why can't you?" demanded Beulah incisively. "He's tied to the bedpost and I have my gun. I can shoot as straight as you can. What harm can he do me in five minutes? Don't be an idiot, Dan."

Meldrum, grumbling, passed into the back room.

In an instant Beulah was at the table, had drawn out a drawer, and had seized a carving knife. She turned on Dingwell, eyes flashing.

"If I help you to escape, will you swear to say nothing that will hurt my father or anybody else in the park?" she demanded in a low voice.

"Yes—if young Beaudry has not been hurt."

"You swear it."

"Yes."

She tossed him the knife, and moved swiftly back to the place where she had been standing. "Whatever my father wants you to do you'd better do," she said out loud for the benefit of Meldrum.

Dingwell cut the ropes that bound his leg. "I'm liable to be Dan's guest quite awhile yet. Rutherford and I don't quite agree on the terms," he drawled aloud.

Beulah tossed him her revolver. "I'll call Dan, but you're not to hurt him," she whispered.

When Meldrum came in answer to her summons, he met the shock of his life. In Dingwell's competent hand was a revolver aimed at his heart.

The man turned savagely to Beulah. "So I'm the goat," he said with a curse. "Rutherford is going to frame me, is he? I'm to go to the pen in place of the whole bunch. Is that it?"

"No, you've guessed wrong. Yore hide is safe this time, Meldrum," the cattleman explained. "Reach for the roof. No, don't do that. . . . Now, turn yore face to the wall."

Dave stepped forward and gathered in the forty-four of

the enemy. He also relieved him of his "skinning" knife. With the deft hands of an old roper he tied the man up and flung him on the bed.

This done, Dingwell made straight for the larder. Though he was ravenous, the cattleman ate with discretion. Into his pockets he packed all the sandwiches they would hold.

"Is it true that you—that they didn't give you anything to eat?" asked Beulah.

He looked at her—and lied cheerfully.

"Sho, I got cranky and wouldn't eat. Yore folks treated me fine. I got my neck bowed. Can't blame them for that, can I?"

"We must be going," she told him. "If you don't get over the pass before morning, Tighe might catch you."

He nodded agreement. "You're right, but I've got to look out for young Beaudry. Do you know where he is?"

"He is waiting outside," the girl said stiffly. "Take him away with you. I'll not be responsible for him if he comes back. We don't like spies here."

They found Roy lying against the wall of the hut, his white face shining in the moonlight.

"What's the matter with you?" demanded Miss Rutherford sharply.

"I'm all right." Roy managed to rise and lean against the *jacal.* "I see you made it. Mr. Dingwell, my name is Beaudry."

"Glad to know you." The cattleman's strong hand gripped his limp one. "Yore father was the gamest man I ever knew and one of my best friends."

The keen eyes of Beulah had been fastened on Roy.

She recalled what she had heard the man say in the orchard. In her direct fashion she flung a question at the young man.

"Are you wounded? Did that man hit you when he fired?"

"It's in my shoulder—just a flesh wound. The bleeding has stopped except when I move."

"Why didn't you say something about it?" she asked impatiently. "Do you think we're clairvoyants? We'd better get him into the house and look at it, Mr. Dingwell."

They did as she suggested. A bullet had ploughed a furrow across the shoulder. Except for the loss of blood, the wound was not serious. With the help of Miss Rutherford, which was given as a matter of course and quite without embarrassment, Dave dressed and bandaged the hurt like an expert. In his adventurous life he had looked after many men who had been shot, and had given first aid to a dozen with broken bones.

Roy winced a little at the pain, but he made no outcry. He was not a baby about suffering. That he could stand as well as another. What shook his nerve was the fear of anticipation, the dread of an impending disaster which his imagination magnified.

"You'd better hurry," he urged two or three times. "Some one might come any minute."

Dave looked at him, a little surprised. "What's the urge, son? We've got two six-guns with us if anybody gets too neighborly."

But Beulah was as keen for the start as Beaudry. She did not want the men escaping from the park to meet with her people. To avoid this, rapid travel was necessary.

As soon as Roy was patched up they started.

CHAPTER 14

PERSONALLY ESCORTED

Before they reached the mouth of the cañon, Dave was supporting the slack body of his friend. When the party came to the aspens, Beulah hurried forward, and by the time the two men emerged she was waiting for them with Blacky.

Roy protested at taking the horse, but the girl cut short his objections imperiously.

"Do you think we've only your silly pride to consider? I want you out of the park—where my people can't reach you. I'm going to see you get out. After that I don't care what you do."

Moonlight fell upon the sardonic smile on the pitifully white face of the young man. "I'm to be personally conducted by the Queen of Huerfano. That's great. I certainly appreciate the honor."

With the help of Dingwell he pulled himself to the saddle. The exertion started a spurt of warm blood at the shoulder, but Roy clenched his teeth and clung to the pommel to steady himself. The cattleman led the horse and Beulah walked beside him.

"I can get another pony for you at Cameron's," she explained. "Just above there is a short cut by way of Dolores Sinks. You ought to be across the divide before morning. I'll show you the trail."

What story she told to get the horse from Cameron her companions did not know, but from where they waited in the pines they saw the flickering light of a lantern cross to the stable. Presently Beulah rode up to them on the hillside above the ranch.

By devious paths she led them through chaparral and woodland. Sometimes they followed her over hills and again into gulches. The girl "spelled" Dingwell at riding the second horse, but whether in the saddle or on foot her movements showed such swift certainty that Dave was satisfied she knew where she was going.

Twice she stopped to rest the wounded man, who was now clinging with both hands to the saddle-horn. But the hard gleam of her dark eyes served notice that she was moved by expediency and not sympathy.

It was midnight when at last she stopped near the entrance to the pass.

"The road lies straight before you over the divide. You can't miss it. Once on the other side keep going till you get into the foothills. All trails will take you down," she told Dingwell.

"We're a heap obliged to you, Miss Rutherford," answered Dingwell. "I reckon neither one of us is liable to forget what you've done for us."

She flamed. "I've nothing against you, Mr. Dingwell, but you might as well know that what I've done was for my people. I don't want them to get into trouble. If it hadn't been for that—"

"You'd 'a' done it just the same," the cattleman finished for her with a smile. "You can't make me mad to-night after going the limit for us the way you have."

Beaudry, sagging over the horn of the saddle, added his word timidly, but the Rutherford girl would have none of his thanks.

"You don't owe me anything, I tell you. How many times have I got to say that it is nothing to me what becomes of you?" she replied, flushing angrily. "All I ask is that you don't cross my path again. Next time I'll let Jess Tighe have his way."

"I didn't go into the park to spy on your people, Miss Rutherford. I went to—"

"I care nothing about why you came." The girl turned to Dingwell, her chin in the air. "Better let him rest every mile or two. I don't want him breaking down in our country after all the trouble I've taken."

"You may leave him to me. I'll look out for him," Dave promised.

"Just so that you don't let him get caught again," she added.

Her manner was cavalier, her tone almost savage. Without another word she turned and left them.

Dingwell watched her slim form disappear into the night.

"Did you ever see such a little thoroughbred?" he asked admiringly. "I take off my hat to her. She's the gamest kid I ever met—and pretty as they grow. Just think of her pulling off this getaway to-night. It was a man-size job, and that little girl never turned a hair from start to finish. And loyal! By Gad! Hal Rutherford hasn't earned fidelity like that, even if he has been father and mother to her since she was a year old. He'd ought to send her away from that hell-hole and give her a chance."

"What will they do to her when she gets back?"

Dave chuckled. "They can't do a thing. That's the beauty of it. There'll be a lot of tall cussing in Huerfano for a while, but after Hal has onloaded what's on his chest, he'll stand between her and the rest."

"Sure of that?"

"It's a cinch." The cattleman laughed softly. "But ain't she the little spitfire? I reckon she sure hates you thorough."

Roy did not answer. He was sliding from the back of his horse in a faint.

When Beaudry opened his eyes again, Dingwell was pouring water into his mouth from a canteen that had been hanging to the pommel of Miss Rutherford's saddle.

"Was I unconscious?" asked the young man in disgust.

"That's whatever. Just you lie there, son, whilst I fix these bandages up for you again."

The cattleman moistened the hot cloths with cold water and rearranged them.

"We ought to be hurrying on," Roy suggested, glancing anxiously down the steep ascent up which they had ridden.

"No rush a-tall," Dave assured him cheerfully. "We got all the time there is. Best thing to do is to loaf along and take it easy."

"But they'll be on our trail as soon as they know we've gone. They'll force Miss Rutherford to tell which way we came."

Dingwell grinned. "Son, did you ever look into that girl's eyes? They look right at you, straight and unafraid. The Huerfano Park outfit will have a real merry time getting her to tell anything she doesn't want to. When she gets her neck bowed, I'll bet she's some sot. Might as well argue with a government mule. She'd make a right interesting wife for some man, but he'd have to be a humdinger to hold his end up—six foot of man, lots of patience, and sense enough to know he'd married a woman out of 'steen thousand."

Young Beaudry was not contemplating matrimony. His interest just now was centered in getting as far from the young woman and her relatives as possible.

"When young Rutherford finds he has been sold, there will be the deuce to pay," urged Roy.

"Will there? I dunno. Old man Rutherford ain't going to be so awfully keen to get us back on his hands. We worried him a heap. Miss Beulah lifted two heavy weights off'n his mind. I'm one and you're the other. O' course, he'll start the boys out after us to square himself with Tighe and Meldrum. He's got to do that. They're sure going to be busy bees down in the Huerfano hive. The Rutherford boys are going to do a lot of night-riding for quite some time. But I expect Hal won't give them orders to bring us in dead or alive. There is no premium on our pelts."

Roy spent a nervous half-hour before his friend would let him mount again—and he showed it. The shrewd eyes of the old cattleman appraised him. Already he guessed some of the secrets of this young man's heart.

Dave swung to the left into the hills so as to get away

from the beaten trails after they had crossed the pass. He rode slowly, with a careful eye upon his companion. Frequently he stopped to rest in spite of Roy's protests.

Late in the afternoon they came to a little mountain ranch owned by a nester who had punched cattle for Dave in the old days. Now he was doing a profitable business himself in other men's calves. He had started with a branding-iron and a flexible conscience. He still had both of them, together with a nice little bunch of cows that beat the world's records for fecundity.

It was not exactly the place Dingwell would have chosen to go into hiding, but he had to take what he could get. Roy, completely exhausted, was already showing a fever. He could not possibly travel farther.

With the casual confidence that was one of his assets Dave swung from his horse and greeted the ranchman.

" 'Lo, Hart! Can we roost here to-night? My friend got thrown and hurt his shoulder. He's all in."

The suspicious eyes of the nester passed over Beaudry and came back to Dingwell.

"I reckon so," he said, not very graciously. "We're not fixed for company, but if you'll put up with what we've got—"

"Suits us fine. My friend's name is Beaudry. I'll get him right to bed."

Roy stayed in bed for forty-eight hours. His wound was only a slight one and the fever soon subsided. The third day he was sunning himself on the porch. Dave had gone on a little jaunt to a water-hole to shoot hooters for supper. Mrs. Hart was baking bread inside. Her husband had left before daybreak and was not yet back. He was looking for strays, his wife said.

In the family rocking-chair Roy was reading a torn copy of "Martin Chuzzlewit." How it had reached this haven was a question, since it was the only book in the house except a Big Creek bible, as the catalogue of a mail-order house is called in that country. Beaudry resented the frank, insolent observations of Dickens on the manners of Americans. In the first place, the types were not true to life. In the second place—

The young man heard footsteps coming around the corner of the house. He glanced up carelessly—and his heart seemed to stop beating.

He was looking into the barrel of a revolver pointed straight at him. Back of the weapon was the brutal, triumphant face of Meldrum. It was set in a cruel grin that showed two rows of broken, tobacco-stained teeth.

"By God! I've got you. Git down on yore knees and beg, Mr. Spy. I'm going to blow yore head off in just thirty seconds."

Not in his most unbridled moments had Dickens painted a bully so appalling as this one. This man was a notorious "killer" and the lust of murder was just now on him. Young Beaudry's brain reeled. It was only by an effort that he pulled himself back from the unconsciousness into which he was swimming.

CHAPTER 15

THE BAD MAN

The eyes of Beaudry, held in dreadful fascination, clung to the lupine face behind the revolver. To save his life he could have looked nowhere else except into those cold, narrow pupils where he read death. Little beads of sweat stood on his forehead. The tongue in his mouth was dry. His brain seemed paralyzed. Again he seemed to be lifted from his feet by a wave of deadly terror.

Meldrum had been drinking heavily, but he was not drunk. He drew from his pocket a watch and laid it on the arm of the chair. Roy noticed that the rim of the revolver did not waver. It was pointed directly between his eyes.

"Git down on yore knees and beg, damn you. In less 'n a minute hell pops for you."

The savage, exultant voice of the former convict beat upon Roy like the blows of a hammer. He would have begged for his life,—begged abjectly, cravenly,—but his teeth chattered and his parched tongue was palsied. He would have sunk to his knees, but terror had robbed his muscles of the strength to move. He was tied to his chair by ropes stronger than chains of steel.

The watch ticked away the seconds. From the face of Meldrum the grin was snuffed out by a swift surge of wolfish anger.

"Are you deef and dumb?" he snarled. "It's Dan Meldrum talking—the man yore dad sent to the penitentiary. I'm going to kill you. Then I'll cut another notch on my gun. Understand?"

The brain of the young lawyer would not function. His will was paralyzed. Yet every sense was amazingly alert. He did not miss a tick of the watch. Every beat of his heart registered.

"You butted in and tried to spy like yore dad, did you?" the raucous voice continued. "Thought you could sell us out and git away with it. Here's where you learn different. Jack Beaudry was a man, anyhow, and we got him. You're nothing but a pink-ear, a whey-faced baby without guts to stand the gaff. Well, you've come to the end of yore trail. Beg, you skunk!"

From the mind of Beaudry the fog lifted. In the savage, malignant eyes glaring at him he read that he was lost. The clutch of fear so overwhelmed him that suspense was unbearable. He wanted to shriek aloud, to call on this man-killer to end the agony. It was the same impulse, magnified a hundred times, that leads a man to bite on an ulcerated tooth in a weak impotence of pain.

The tick-tick-tick of the watch mocked him to frenzied action. He gripped the arms of the chair with both hands and thrust forward his face against the cold rim of the revolver barrel.

"Shoot!" he cried hoarsely, drunk with terror. "Shoot, and be damned!"

Before the words were out of his mouth a shot echoed. For the second time in his life Roy lost consciousness. Not many seconds could have passed before he opened his eyes again. But what he saw puzzled him.

Meldrum was writhing on the ground and cursing. His left hand nursed the right, which moved up and down frantically as if to escape from pain. Toward the house walked Dingwell and by his side Beulah Rutherford. Dave was ejecting a shell from the rifle he carried. Slowly it came to the young man that he had not been shot. The convict must have been hit instead by a bullet from the gun of the cattleman. He was presently to learn that the forty-four had been struck and knocked from the hand of its owner.

"Every little thing all right, son?" asked the cowman cheerily. "We sure did run this rescue business fine. Another minute and—But what's the use of worrying? Miss Beulah and I were Johnny-on-the-spot all right."

Roy said nothing. He could not speak. His lips and cheeks were still bloodless. By the narrowest margin in the world he had escaped.

Disgustedly the cattleman looked down at Meldrum, who was trying to curse and weep from pain at the same time.

"Stung you up some, did I? Hm! You ought to be singing hymns because I didn't let you have it in the haid, which I'd most certainly have done if you had harmed my friend. Get up, you bully, and stop cursing. There's a lady here, and you ain't damaged, anyhow."

The eyes of Beaudry met those of Beulah. It seemed to him that her lip curled contemptuously. She had been witness of his degradation, had seen him show the white feather. A pulse of shame beat in his throat.

"W-w-what are you doing here?" he asked wretchedly.

Dave answered for her. "Isn't she always on the job when she's needed? Yore fairy godmother—that's what Miss Beulah Rutherford is. Rode hell-for-leather down here to haid off that coyote there—and done it, too. Bumped into me at the water-hole and I hopped on that Blacky hawss behind her. He brought us in on the jump and Sharps old reliable upset Meldrum's apple cart."

Still nursing the tips of his tingling fingers, the ex-convict scowled venomously at Beulah. "I'll remember that, missie. That's twice you've interfered with me. I sure will learn you to mind yore own business."

Dingwell looked steadily at him. "We've heard about enough from you. Beat it! Hit the trail! Pull yore freight! Light out! *Vamos!* Git!"

The man-killer glared at him. For a moment he hesitated. He would have liked to try conclusions with the cattleman to a fighting finish, but though he had held his own in many a rough-and-tumble fray, he lacked the unflawed nerve to face this man with the cold gray eye and the chilled-steel jaw. His fury broke in an impotent curse as he slouched away.

"I don't understand yet," pursued Roy. "How did Miss Rutherford know that Meldrum was coming here?"

"Friend Hart rode up to tell Tighe we were here. He met Meldrum close to the schoolhouse. The kids were playing hide-and-go-seek. One of them was lying right back of a big rock beside the road. He heard Dan swear he was coming down to stop yore clock, son. The kid went straight to teacher soon as the men had ridden off. He told what Meldrum had said. So, of course, Miss Beulah she sent the children home and rode down to the hawss ranch to get her father or one of her brothers. None of them were at home and she hit the trail alone to warn us."

"I knew my people would be blamed for what this man did, so I blocked him," explained the girl with her habitual effect of hostile pride.

"You said you would let Tighe have his way next time, but you don't need to apologize for breaking yore word, Miss Beulah," responded Dingwell with his friendly smile. "All we've got to say is that you've got chalked up against us an account we'll never be able to pay."

The color beat into her cheeks. She was both embarrassed and annoyed. With a gesture of impatience she turned away and walked to Blacky. Lithely she swung to the saddle.

Mrs. Hart had come to the porch. In her harassed countenance still lingered the remains of good looks. The droop at the corners of her mouth suggested a faint resentment against a fate which had stolen her youth without leaving the compensations of middle life.

"Won't you light off'n yore bronc and stay to supper, Miss Rutherford?" she invited.

"Thank you, Mrs. Hart. I can't. Must get home."

With a little nod to the woman she swung her horse around and was gone.

Hart did not show up for supper nor for breakfast. It was an easy guess that he lacked the hardihood to face them after his attempted betrayal. At all events, they saw nothing of him before they left in the morning. If they had penetrated his wife's tight-lipped reserve, they might have shared her opinion, that he had gone off on a long drinking-bout with Dan Meldrum.

Leisurely Beaudry and his friend rode down through the chaparral to Battle Butte.

On the outskirts of the town they met Ned Rutherford. After they had passed him, he turned and followed in their tracks.

Dingwell grinned across at Roy. "Some thorough our friends are. A bulldog has got nothing on them. They're hanging around to help me dig up that gunnysack when I get ready."

The two men rode straight to the office of the sheriff and had a talk with him. From there they went to the hotel where Dave usually put up when he was in town. Over their dinner the cattleman renewed an offer he had been urging upon Roy all the way down from Hart's place. He needed a reliable man to help him manage the different holdings he had been accumulating. His proposition was to take Beaudry in as a junior partner, the purchase price to be paid in installments to be earned out of the profits of the business.

" 'Course I don't want to take you away from the law if you're set on that profession, but if you don't really care—" Dave lifted an eyebrow in a question.

"I think I'd like the law, but I know I would like better an active outdoor life. That's not the point, Mr. Dingwell. I can't take something for nothing. You can get a hundred men who know far more about cattle than I do. Why do you pick me?"

"I've got reasons a-plenty. Right off the bat here are some of them. I'm under obligations to Jack Beaudry and I'd like to pay my debt to his son. I've got no near kin of my own. I need a partner, but it isn't one man out of a dozen I can get along with. Most old cowmen are rutted in their ways. You don't know a thing about the business. But you can learn. You're teachable. You are not one of these wise guys. Then, too, I like you, son. I don't want a partner that rubs me the wrong way. Hell, my whyfors all simmer down to one. You're the partner I want, Roy."

"If you find I don't suit you, will you let me know?"

"Sure. But there is no chance of that." Dave shook hands with him joyously. "It's a deal, boy."

"It's a deal," agreed Beaudry.

CHAPTER 16

ROY IS INVITED TO TAKE A DRINK

Dingwell gave a fishing-party next day. His invited guests were Sheriff Sweeney, Royal Beaudry, Pat Ryan, and Superintendent Elder, of the Western Express Company. Among those present, though at a respectful distance, were Ned Rutherford and Brad Charlton.

The fishermen took with them neither rods nor bait. Their flybooks were left at home. Beaudry brought to the meeting-place a quarter-inch rope and a grappling-iron with three hooks. Sweeney and Ryan carried rifles and the rest of the party revolvers.

Dave himself did the actual fishing. After the grappling-hook had been attached to the rope, he dropped it into Big Creek from a large rock under the bridge that leads to town from Lonesome Park. He hooked his big fish at the fourth cast and worked it carefully into the shallow water. Roy waded into the stream and dragged the catch ashore. It proved to be a gunnysack worth twenty thousand dollars.

Elder counted the sacks inside. "Everything is all right. How did you come to drop the money here?"

"I'm mentioning no names, Mr. Elder. But I was so fixed that I couldn't turn back. If I left the road, my tracks would show. There were reasons why I didn't want to continue on into town with the loot. So, as I was crossing the bridge, without leaving the saddle or even stopping, I deposited the gold in the Big Creek safety deposit vault," Dingwell answered with a grin.

"But supposing the Rutherfords had found it?" The superintendent put his question blandly.

The face of the cattleman was as expressive as a stone wall. "Did I mention the Rutherfords?" he asked, looking straight into the eye of the Western Express man. "I reckon you didn't hear me quite right."

Elder laughed a little. He was a Westerner himself. "Oh, I heard you, Mr. Dingwell. But I haven't heard a lot of things I'd like to know."

The cattleman pushed the sack with his toe. "Money talks, folks say."

"Maybe so. But it hasn't told me why you couldn't go back along the road you came, why you couldn't leave the road, and why you didn't want to go right up to Sweeney's office with the sack. It hasn't given me any information about where you have been the past two weeks, or how—"

"My gracious! He bubbles whyfors and howfors like he had just come uncorked," murmured Dave, in his slow drawl. "Just kinder effervesces them out of the mouth."

"I know you're not going to tell me anything you don't want me to know, still—"

"You done guessed it first crack. Move on up to the haid of the class."

"Still, you can't keep me from thinking. You can call the turn on the fellows that robbed the Western Express Company whenever you feel like it. Right now you could name the men that did it."

Dave's most friendly, impudent smile beamed upon the superintendent. "I thank you for the compliment, Mr. Elder. Honest, I didn't know how smart a haid I had in my hat till you told me."

"It's good ye've got an air-tight alibi yoursilf, Dave," grinned Pat Ryan.

"I've looked up his alibi. It will hold water," admitted Elder genially. "Well, Dingwell, if you won't talk, you won't. We'll move on up to the bank and deposit our find. Then the drinks will be on me."

The little procession moved uptown. A hundred yards behind it came young Rutherford and Charlton as a rear guard. When the contents of the sack had been put in a vault for safe-keeping, Elder invited the party into the Last Chance. Dave and Roy ordered buttermilk.

Dingwell gave his partner a nudge. "See who is here."

The young man nodded gloomily. He had recognized already the two men drinking at a table in the rear.

"Meldrum and Hart make a sweet pair to draw to when they're tanking up. They're about the two worst bad men in this part of the country. My advice is to take the other side of the street when you see them coming," Ryan contributed.

The rustlers glowered at Elder's party, but offered no comment other than some sneering laughter and ribald whispering. Yet Beaudry breathed freer when he was out in the open again lengthening the distance between him and them at every stride.

Ryan walked as far as the hotel with Dave and his partner.

"Come in and have dinner with us, Pat," invited the cattleman.

The Irishman shook his head. "Can't, Dave. Got to go round to the Elephant Corral and look at my horse. A nail wint into its foot last night."

After they had dined, Dingwell looked at his watch. "I want you to look over the ranch to-day, son. We'll ride out and I'll show you the place. But first I've got to register a kick with the station agent about the charges for freight on a wagon I had shipped in from Denver. Will you stop at Salmon's and order this bill of groceries sent up to the corral? I'll meet you here at 2:30."

Roy walked up Mission Street as far as Salmon's New York Grocery and turned in the order his friend had given him. After he had seen it filled, he strolled along the sunny street toward the plaza. It was one of those warm, somnolent New Mexico days as peaceful as old age. Burros blinked sleepily on three legs and a hoof-tip. Cowponies switched their tails indolently to brush away flies. An occasional half-garbed Mexican lounged against a door jamb or squatted in the shade of a wall. A squaw from the reservation crouched on the curb beside her display of pottery. Not a sound disturbed the siesta of Battle Butte.

Into this peace broke an irruption of riot. A group of men poured through the swinging doors of a saloon into the open arcade in front. Their noisy disputation shattered the sunny stillness like a fusillade in the desert. Plainly they were much the worse for liquor.

Roy felt again the familiar clutch at his throat, the ice drench at his heart, and the faint slackness of his leg muscles. For in the crowd just vomited from the Silver Dollar were Meldrum, Fox, Hart, Charlton, and Ned Rutherford.

Charlton it was that caught sight of the passing man. With an exultant whoop he leaped out, seized Beaudry, and swung him into the circle of hillmen.

"Tickled to death to meet up with you, Mr. Royal-Cherokee-Beaudry-Street. How is every little thing a-coming? Fine as silk, eh? You'd ought to be laying by quite a bit of the mazuma, what with rewards and spy money together," taunted Charlton.

To the center of the circle Meldrum elbowed his drunken way. "Lemme get at the pink-ear. Lemme bust him one," he demanded.

Ned Rutherford held him back. "Don't break yore breeching, Dan. Brad has done spoke for him," the young man drawled.

Into the white face of his victim Charlton puffed the smoke of his cigar. "If you ain't too busy going fishing maybe you could sell me a windmill to-day. How about that, Mr. Cornell-I-Yell?"

"Where's yore dry nurse Dingwell?" broke in the ex-convict bitterly. "Thought he tagged you everywhere. Tell the son-of-a-gun for me that next time we meet I'll curl his hair right."

Roy said nothing. He looked wildly around for a way of escape and found none. A half ring of jeering faces walled him from the street.

"Lemme get at him. Lemme crack him one on the bean," insisted Meldrum as he made a wild pass at Beaudry.

"No hurry a-tall," soothed Ned. "We got all evening before us. Take yore time, Dan."

"Looks to me like it's certainly up to Mr. Cherokee-What's-his-name-Beaudry to treat the crowd," suggested Chet Fox.

The young man clutched at the straw. "Sure. Of course I will. Glad to treat, even though I don't drink myself," he said with a weak, forced heartiness.

"You *don't* drink. The hell you don't!" cut in Meldrum above the Babel of voices.

"He drinks—hic—buttermilk," contributed Hart.

"He'll drink whiskey when I give the word, by Gad!" Meldrum shook himself free of Rutherford and pressed forward. He dragged a bottle from his pocket, drew out the cork, and thrust the liquor at Roy. "Drink, you yellow-streaked coyote—and drink a-plenty."

Roy shook his head. "No—no!" he protested. "I—I—never touch it." His lips were ashen. The color had fled from his cheeks.

The desperado pushed his cruel, vice-scarred face close to that of the man he hated.

"Sa-ay. Listen to me, young fellow. I'm going to bump you off one o' these days sure. Me, I don't like yore name nor the color of yore hair nor the map you wear for a face. I'm a killer. Me, Dan Meldrum. And I serve notice on you right now." With an effort he brought his mind back to the issue on hand. "But that ain't the point. When I ask a man to drink he drinks. See? You ain't deef, are you? Then drink, you rabbit!"

Beaudry, his heart beating like a triphammer, told himself that he was not going to drink—that they could not make him—that he would die first. But before he knew it the flask was in his trembling fingers. Apparently, without the consent of his flaccid will, the muscles had responded to the impulse of obedience to the spur of fear. Even while his brain drummed the refrain, "I won't drink—I won't—I won't," the bottle was rising to his lips.

He turned a ghastly grin on his tormentors. It was meant to propitiate them, to save the last scrap of his self-respect by the assumption that they were all good fellows together. Feebly it suggested that after all a joke is a joke.

From the uptilted flask the whiskey poured into his mouth. He swallowed, and the fiery liquid scorched his throat. Before he could hand the liquor back to its owner, the ex-convict broke into a curse.

"Drink, you pink-ear. Don't play 'possum with me," he roared. Roy drank. Swallow after swallow of the stuff burned its way into his stomach. He stopped at last, sputtering and coughing.

"M—much obliged. I'll be going now," he stammered.

"Not quite yet, Mr. R. C. Street-Beaudry," demurred Charlton suavely. "Stay and play with us awhile, now you're here. No telling when we'll meet again." He climbed on the shoe-shining chair that stood in the entry. “I reckon I’ll have my boots shined up. Go to it, Mr. Beaudry-Street.”

With a whoop of malice the rest of them fell in with the suggestion. To make this young fellow black their boots in turn was the most humiliating thing they could think of at the moment. They pushed Roy toward the stand and put a brush into his hand. He stood still, hesitating.

“Git down on yore knees and hop to it,” ordered Charlton. “Give him room, boys.”

Again Beaudry swore to himself that he would not do it. He had an impulse to smash that sneering, cruel face, but it was physically impossible for him to lift a hand to strike. Though he was trembling violently, he had no intention of yielding. Yet the hinges of his knees bent automatically. He found himself reaching for the blacking just as if his will were paralyzed.

Perhaps it was liquor rushing to his head when he stooped. Perhaps it was the madness of a terror-stricken rat driven into a corner. His fear broke bounds, leaped into action. Beaudry saw red. With both hands he caught Charlton’s foot, twisted it savagely, and flung the man head over heels out of the chair. He snatched up the boot-black’s stool by one leg and brought it crashing down on the head of Meldrum. The ex-convict went down as if he had been pole-axed.

There was no time to draw guns, no time to prepare a defense. His brain on fire from the liquor he had drunk and his overpowering terror, Beaudry was a berserk gone mad with the lust of battle. He ran amuck like a maniac, using the stool as a weapon to hammer down the heads of his foes. It crashed first upon one, now on another.

Charlton rushed him and was struck down beside Meldrum. Hart, flung back into the cigar-case, smashed the glass into a thousand splinters. Young Rutherford was sent spinning into the street.

His assailants gave way before Beaudry, at first slowly, then in a panic of haste to escape. He drove them to the sidewalk, flailing away at those within reach. Chet Fox hurdled in his flight a burro loaded with wood.

Then, suddenly as it had swept over Roy, the brainstorm passed. The mists cleared from his eyes. He looked down at the leg of the stool in his hand, which was all that remained of it. He looked up—and saw Beulah Rutherford in the street astride a horse.

She spoke to her brother, who had drawn a revolver from his pocket. "You don't need that now, Ned. He's through."

Her contemptuous voice stung Roy. "Why didn't they leave me alone, then?" he said sullenly in justification.

The girl did not answer him. She slipped from the horse and ran into the arcade with the light grace that came of perfect health and the freedom of the hills. The eyes of the young man followed this slim, long-limbed Diana as she knelt beside Charlton and lifted his bloody head into her arms. He noticed that her eyes burned and that her virginal bosom rose and fell in agitation.

None the less she gave first aid with a business-like economy of motion. "Bring water, Ned,—and a doctor," she snapped crisply, her handkerchief pressed against the wound.

To see what havoc he had wrought amazed Roy. The arcade looked as if a cyclone had swept through it. The cigar-stand was shattered beyond repair, its broken glass strewn everywhere. The chair of the bootblack had been splintered into kindling wood. Among the debris sat Meldrum groaning, both hands pressing a head that furiously ached. Brad Charlton was just beginning to wake up to his surroundings.

A crowd had miraculously gathered from nowhere. The fat marshal of Battle Butte was puffing up the street a block away. Beaudry judged it time to be gone. He dropped the leg of the stool and strode toward the hotel.

Already his fears were active again. What would the hillmen do to him when they had recovered from the panic into which his madness had thrown them? Would they start for him at once? Or would they mark one more score against him and wait? He could scarcely keep his feet from breaking into a run to get more quickly from the vicinity of the Silver Dollar. He longed mightily to reach the protection of Dave Dingwell's experience and debonair *sang-froid.*

The cattleman had not yet reached the hotel. Roy went up to their room at once and locked himself in. He sat on the bed with a revolver in his hand. Now that it was all over, he was trembling like an aspen leaf. For the hundredth time in the past week he flung at himself his own contemptuous scorn. Why was the son of John Beaudry such an arrant coward? He knew that his sudden madness and its consequences had been born of panic. What was there about the quality of his nerves that differed from those of other men? Even now he was shivering from the dread that his enemies might come and break down the door to get at him.

He heard the jocund whistle of Dingwell as the cattleman came along the corridor. Swiftly he pocketed the revolver and unlocked the door. When Dave entered, Roy was lying on the bed pretending to read a newspaper.

If the older man noticed that the paper shook, he ignored it.

"What's this I hear, son, about you falling off the water-wagon and filling the hospital?" His gay grin challenged affectionately the boy on the bed. "Don't you know you're liable to give the new firm, Dingwell & Beaudry, a bad name if you pull off insurrections like that? The city dads are talking some of building a new wing to the accident ward to accommodate your victims. Taxes will go up and—"

Roy smiled wanly. "You've heard about it, then?"

"Heard about it! Say, son, I've heard nothing else for the last twenty minutes. You're the talk of the town. I didn't know you was such a bad actor." Dave stopped to break into a chuckle. "Wow! You certainly hit the high spots. Friend Meldrum and Charlton and our kind host Hart—all laid out at one clatter. I never was lucky. Here I wouldn't 'a' missed seeing you pull off this Samson encore for three cows on the hoof, and I get in too late for the show."

"They're not hurt badly, are they?" asked Beaudry, a little timidly.

Dave looked at him with a curious little smile. "You don't want to go back and do the job more thorough, do you? No need, son. Meldrum and Charlton are being patched up in the hospital and Hart is at Doc White's having the glass picked out of his geography. I've talked with some of the also rans, and they tell me unanimous that it was the most thorough clean-up they have participated in recently."

"What will they do—after they get over it?"

Dingwell grinned. "Search me! But I'll tell you what they won't do. They'll not invite you to take another drink right away. I'll bet a hat on that. . . . Come on, son. We got to hit the trail for home."

CHAPTER 17

ROY IMPROVES THE SHINING HOURS

The tender spring burnt into crisp summer. Lean hill cattle that had roughed through the winter storms lost their shaggy look and began to fill out. For there had been early rains and the bunch grass was succulent this year.

Roy went about learning his new business with an energy that delighted his partner. He was eager to learn and was not too proud to ask questions. The range conditions, the breeding of cattle, and transportation problems were all studied by him. Within a month or two he had become a fair horseman and could rope a steer inexpertly.

Dingwell threw out a suggestion one day in his characteristic casual manner. The two men were riding a line fence and Roy had just missed a shot at a rabbit.

"Better learn to shoot, son. Take an hour off every day and practice. You hadn't ought to have missed that cottontail. What you want is to fire accurately, just as soon as yore gun jumps to the shoulder. I can teach you a wrinkle or two with a six-gun. Then every time you see a rattler, take a crack at it. Keep in form. *You might need to bend a gun one of these days.*"

His partner understood what that last veiled allusion meant. The weeks had slipped away since the fracas in front of the Silver Dollar. The enemy had made no move. But cowpunchers returning to the ranch from town reported that both Meldrum and Charlton had sworn revenge. It was an even bet that either one of them would shoot on sight.

Beaudry took Dave's advice. Every day he rode out to a wash and carried with him a rifle and a revolver. He practiced for rapidity as well as accuracy. He learned how to fire from the hip, how to empty a revolver in less than two seconds, how to shoot lying down, and how to hit a mark either from above or below.

The young man never went to town alone. He stuck close to the ranch. The first weeks had been full of stark terror lest he might find one of his enemies waiting for him behind a clump of prickly pear or hidden in the mesquite of some lonely wash. He was past that stage, but his nerves were still jumpy. It was impossible for him to forget that at least three men were deadly enemies of his and would stamp out his life as they would that of a wolf. Each morning he wakened with a little shock of dread. At night he breathed relief for a few hours of safety.

Meanwhile Dave watched him with an indolent carelessness of manner that masked his sympathy. If it had been possible, he would have taken the burden on his own broad, competent shoulders. But this was not in Dingwell's code. He had been brought up in that outdoor school of the West where a man has to game out his own feuds. As the cattleman saw it, Roy had to go through now just as his father had done seventeen years before.

In town one day Dave met Pat Ryan and had a talk with him over dinner. A remark made by the little cowpuncher surprised his friend. Dingwell looked at him with narrowed, inquiring eyes.

The Irishman nodded. "Ye thought you were the only one that knew it? Well, I'm on, too, Dave."

"That's not what I hear everywhere else, Pat," answered the cattleman, still studying the other. "Go down the street and mention the name of Royal Beaudry—ask any one if he is game. What will you get for a reply?"

Without the least hesitation Ryan spoke out. "You'll hear that he's got more guts than any man in Washington County—that he doesn't know what fear is. Then likely you'll be told it's natural enough, since he's the son of Jack Beaudry, the fighting sheriff. Ever-rybody believes that excipt you and me, Dave. We know better."

"What do we know, Pat?"

"We know that the bye is up against a man-size job and is scared stiff."

"Hmp! Was he scared when he licked a dozen men at the Silver Dollar and laid out for repairs three of the best fighters in New Mexico?"

"You're shouting right he was, Dave. No man alive could 'a' done it if he hadn't been crazy with fright."

Dingwell laughed. "Hope I'm that way, then, when I get into my next tight place." He added after a moment: "The trouble with the boy is that he has too much imagination. He makes his own private little hell beforehand."

"I reckon he never learned to ride herd on his fears."

"Jack Beaudry told me about him onc't. The kid was born after his mother had been worrying herself sick about Jack. She never could tell when he'd be brought home dead. Well, Roy inherited fear. I've noticed that when a sidewinder rattles, he jumps. Same way, when any one comes up and surprises him. It's what you might call constitootional with him."

"Yep. That's how I've got it figured. But—" Pat hesitated and looked meditatively out of the window.

"All right. Onload yore mind. Gimme the run of the pen just as yore thoughts happen," suggested the cattleman.

"Well, I'm thinking that he's been lucky, Dave. But soon as Tighe's tools guess what we know, something's going to happen to Beaudry. He's got them buffaloed now. But Charlton and Meldrum ain't going to quit. Can you tell me how your friend will stand the acid test next time hell pops?"

Dave shook his head. "I cannot. That's just what is worrying me. There are men that have to be lashed on by ridicule to stand the gaff. But Roy is not like that. I reckon he's all the time flogging himself like the *penitentes.* He's sick with shame because he can't go out grinning to meet his troubles. . . . There ain't a thing I can do for him. He's got to play out his hand alone."

"Sure he has, and if the luck breaks right, I wouldn't put it past him to cash in a winner. He's gamer than most of us because he won't quit even when the divvle of terror is riding his back."

"Another point in his favor is that he learns easily. When he first came out to the Lazy Double D, he was afraid of horses. He has got over that. Give him another month and he'll be a pretty fair shot. Up till the time he struck this country, Roy had lived a soft city life. He's beginning to toughen. The things that scare a man are those that are mysteries to him. Any kid will fight his own brother because he knows all about him, but he's plumb shy about tackling a strange boy. Well, that's how it is with Roy. He has got the notion that Meldrum and Charlton are terrors, but now he has licked them onc't, he won't figure them out as so bad."

"He didn't exactly lick them in a stand-up fight, Dave."

"No, he just knocked them down and tromped on them and put them out of business," agreed Dingwell dryly.

The eyes of the little Irishman twinkled. "Brad Charlton is giving it out that it was an accident."

"That's what I'd call it, too, if I was Brad," assented the cattleman with a grin. "But if we could persuade Roy to put over about one more accident like that, I reckon Huerfano Park would let him alone."

"While Jess Tighe is living?"

Dingwell fell grave. "I'd forgotten Tighe. No, I expect the kid had better keep his weather eye peeled as long as that castor-oil smile of Jess' is working."

CHAPTER 18

RUTHERFORD ANSWERS QUESTIONS

Beulah Rutherford took back with her to Huerfano Park an almost intolerable resentment against the conditions of her life. She had the family capacity for sullen silence, and for weeks a kind of despairing rage simmered in her heart. She was essentially of a very direct, simple nature, clear as Big Creek where it tumbled down from the top of the world toward the foothills. An elemental honesty stirred in her. It was necessary to her happiness that she keep her own self-respect and be able to approve those she loved.

Just now she could do neither. The atmosphere of the ranch seemed to stifle her. When she rode out into a brave, clean world of sunshine, the girl carried her shame along. Ever since she could remember, outlaws and miscreants had slipped furtively about the suburbs of her life. The Rutherfords themselves were a hard and savage breed. To their door had come more than one night rider flying for his life, and Beulah had accepted the family tradition of hospitality to those at odds with society.

A fierce, untamed girl of primitive instincts, she was the heritor of the family temperament. But like threads of gold there ran through the warp of her being a fineness that was her salvation. She hated passionately cruelty and falsehood and deceit. All her life she had walked near pitch and had never been defiled.

Hal Rutherford was too close to her not to feel the estrangement of her spirit. He watched her anxiously, and at last one morning he spoke. She was standing on the porch waiting for Jeff to bring Blacky when Rutherford came out and put his arm around her shoulder.

"What is it, honey?" he asked timidly.

"It's—everything," she answered, her gaze still on the distant hills.

"You haven't quarreled with Brad?"

"No—and I'm not likely to if he'll let me alone."

Her father did not press the point. If Brad and she had fallen out, the young man would have to make his own *amende.*

"None of the boys been deviling you?"

"No."

"Aren't you going to tell dad about it, Boots?"

Presently her dark eyes swept round to his. "Why did you say that you didn't know anything about the Western Express robbery?"

He looked steadily at her. "I didn't say that, Beulah. What I said was that I didn't know where the stolen gold was hidden—and I didn't."

"That was just an evasion. You meant me to think that we had had nothing to do with the—the robbery."

"That's right. I did."

"And all the time—" She broke off, a sob choking her throat.

"I knew who did it. That's correct. But I wasn't a party to the robbery. I knew nothing about it till afterward."

"I've always believed everything you've told me,

dad. And now—"

He felt doubt in her shaken voice. She did not know what to think now. Rutherford set himself to clear away her suspicions. He chose to do it by telling the exact truth.

"Now you may still believe me, honey. The robbery was planned by Tighe. I'll not mention the names of those in it. The day after it was pulled off, I heard of it for the first time. Dave Dingwell knew too much. To protect my friends I had to bring him up here. Legally I'm guilty of abduction and of the train robbery, too, because I butted in after the hold-up and protected the guilty ones. I even tried to save for them the gold they had taken."

"Were—any of the boys in it, dad?" she quavered.

"One of them. I won't tell you which."

"And Brad?"

"We're not giving names, Boots."

"Oh, well! I know he was one of them." She slipped her arm within her father's and gave his hand a little pressure. "I'm glad you told me, just the same, dad. I'd been thinking—worse things about you."

"That's all right, honey. Now you won't worry any more, will you?"

"I don't know. . . . That's not all that troubles me. I feel bad when the boys drink and brawl. That attack on Mr. Beaudry at Battle Butte was disgraceful," she flamed. "I don't care if he did come up here spying. Why can't they let him alone?"

He passed a hand in a troubled fashion through his grizzled hair. "You can bet our boys won't touch him again, Boots. I've laid the law down. But I can't answer for Tighe. He'll do him a meanness if he can, and he'll do it quicker since I've broken off with him because you helped Dingwell and Beaudry to escape. I don't know about Brad."

"I told Brad if he touched him again, I would never speak to him."

"Maybe that will hold him hitched, then. Anyhow, I'm not going to make the young fellow trouble. I'd rather let sleeping dogs lie."

Beulah pressed her arm against his. "I haven't been fair to you, dad. I might have known you would do right."

"I aim to stay friends with my little girl no matter what happens. Yore mother gave you into my hands when she was dying and I promised to be mother and father to you. Yore own father was my brother Anse. He died before you were born. I've been the only dad you ever had, and I reckon you know you've been more to me than any of my own boys."

"You shouldn't say that," she corrected quickly. "I'm a girl, and, of course, you spoil me more. That's all."

She gave him a ferocious little hug and went quickly into the house. Happiness had swept through her veins like the exquisite flush of dawn. Her lustrous eyes were wells of glad tears.

The owner of the horse ranch stood on the porch and watched a rider coming out of the gulch toward him. The man descended heavily from his horse and moved down the path. Rutherford eyed him grimly.

"Well, I'm back," the dismounted horseman said surlily.

"I see you are."

"Got out of the hospital Thursday."

"Hope you've made up yore mind to behave, Dan."

"It doesn't hurt a man to take a drink onc't in a while."

"Depends on the man. It put you in the hospital."

Meldrum ripped out a sudden oath. "Wait. Just wait till I get that pink-ear. I'll drill him full of holes right."

"By God, you'll not!" Rutherford's voice was like the snap of a whip. "Try it. Try it. I'll hunt you down like a wolf and riddle yore carcass."

In amazement the ex-convict stared at him. "What's ailin' you, Rutherford?"

"I'm through with you and Tighe. You'll stop making trouble or you'll get out of here. I'm going to clean up the park—going to make it a place where decent folks can live. You've got yore warning now, Dan. Walk a straight chalk-line or hit the trail."

"You can't talk that way to me, Rutherford. I know too much," threatened Meldrum, baring his teeth.

"Don't think it for a minute, Dan. Who is going to take yore word against mine? I've got the goods on you. I can put you through for rustling any time I have a mind to move. And if you don't let young Beaudry alone, I'll do it."

"Am I the only man that ever rustled? Ain't there others in the park? I reckon you've done some night-riding yore own self."

"Some," drawled Rutherford, with a grim little smile. "By and large, I've raised a considerable crop of hell. But I'm reforming in my old age. New Mexico has had a change of heart. Guns are going out, Meldrum, and little red schoolhouses are coming in. We've got to keep up with the fashions."

"Hmp! Schoolhouses! I know what's ailin' you. Since Anse Rutherford's girl—"

"You're off the reservation, Dan," warned the rancher, and again his low voice had the sting of cactus thorns in it.

Meldrum dropped that subject promptly. "Is Buck going to join this Sunday-School of yours?" he jeered. "And all the boys?"

"That's the programme. Won't you come in, too?"

"And Jess Tighe. He'll likely be one of the teachers."

"You'd better ask him. He hasn't notified me."

"Hell! You and yore kin have given the name to deviltry in this country. Mothers scare their kids by telling them the Rutherfords will git them."

"Fact. But that's played out. My boys are grown up and are at the turn of the trail. It hit me plumb in the face when you fools pulled off that express robbery. It's a piece of big luck you're not all headed for the penitentiary. I know when I've had enough. So now I quit."

"All right. Quit. But we haven't all got to go to the mourner's bench with you, have we? You can travel yore trail and we can go ours, can't we?"

"Not when we're on the same range, Dan. What I say goes." The eyes of Rutherford bored into the cruel little shifty ones of the bad man. "Take your choice, Dan. It's quit yore deviltry or leave this part of the country."

"Who elected you czar of Huerfano Park?" demanded Meldrum, furious with anger.

He glared at the ranchman impotently, turned away with a mumbled oath, and went back with jingling spurs to his horse.

CHAPTER 19

BEAUDRY BLOWS A SMOKE WREATH

Royal Beaudry carried about with him in his work on the Lazy Double D persistent memories of the sloe-eyed gypsy who had recently played so large a part in his life. Men of imagination fall in love, not with a woman, but with the mystery they make of her. The young cattleman was not yet a lover, but a rumor of the future began to murmur in his ears. Beulah Rutherford was on the surface very simple and direct, but his thoughts were occupied with the soul of her. What was the girl like whose actions functioned in courage and independence and harsh hostility?

Life had imposed on her a hard finish. But it was impossible for Roy to believe that this slender, tawny child of the wind and the sun could at heart be bitter and suspicious. He had seen the sweet look of her dark-lashed eyes turned in troubled appeal upon her father. There had been one hour when he had looked into her face and found it radiant, all light and response and ecstasy. The emotion that had pulsed through her then had given the lie to the sullen silence upon which she fell back as a defense. If the gods were good to her some day, the red flower of passion would bloom on her cheeks and the mists that dulled her spirit would melt in the warm sunshine of love.

So the dreamer wove the web of his fancy about her, and the mystery that was Beulah Rutherford lay near his thoughts when he walked or rode or ate or talked.

Nor did it lessen his interest in her that he felt she despised him. The flash of her scornful eyes still stung him. He was beyond caring whether she thought him a spy. He knew that the facts justified him in his attempt to save Dingwell. But he writhed that she should believe him a coward. It came too close home. And since the affray in the arcade, no doubt she set him down, too, as a drunken rowdy.

He made the usual vain valorous resolutions of youth to show her his heroic quality. These served at least one good purpose. If he could not control his fears, he could govern his actions. Roy forced himself by sheer will power to ride alone into Battle Butte once a week. Without hurry he went about his business up and down Mission Street.

The town watched him and commented. "Got sand in his craw, young Beaudry has," was the common verdict. Men wondered what would happen when he met Charlton and Meldrum. Most of them would have backed John Beaudry's son both in their hopes and in their opinion of the result.

Into saloons and gambling-houses word was carried, and from there to the hillmen of the park by industrious peddlers of trouble, that the young cattleman from the Lazy Double D could be found by his enemies heeled for business whenever they wanted him.

Charlton kept morosely to the park. If he had had

nothing to consider except his own inclination, he would have slapped the saddle upon a cowpony and ridden in to Battle Butte at once. But Beulah had laid an interdict upon him. For a year he had been trying to persuade her to marry him, and he knew that he must say good-bye to his hopes if he fought with his enemy.

It was fear that kept Meldrum at home. He had been a killer, but the men he had killed had been taken at a disadvantage. It was one thing to shoot this Beaudry cub down from ambush. It was another to meet him in the open. Moreover, he knew the Rutherfords. The owner of the horse ranch had laid the law down to him. No chance shot from the chaparral was to cut down Dingwell's partner.

The ex-convict listened to the whispers of Tighe. He brooded over them, but he did not act on them. His alcohol-dulled brain told him that he had reached the limit of public sufferance. One more killing by him, and he would pay the penalty at the hands of the law. When he took his revenge, it must be done so secretly that no evidence could connect him with the crime. He must, too, have an alibi acceptable to Hal Rutherford.

Meldrum carried with him to Battle Butte, on his first trip after the arcade affair, a fixed determination to avoid Beaudry. In case he met him, he would pass without speaking.

But all of Meldrum's resolutions were apt to become modified by subsequent inhibitions. In company with one or two cronies he made a tour of the saloons of the town. At each of them he said, "Have another," and followed his own advice to show good faith.

On one of these voyages from port to port the bad man from Chicito Cañon sighted a tall, lean-flanked, long-legged brown man. He was crossing the street so that the party came face to face with him at the apex of a right angle. The tanned stranger in corduroys, hickory shirt, and pinched-in hat of the range rider was Royal Beaudry. It was with a start of surprise that Meldrum recognized him. His enemy was no longer a "pink-ear." There was that in his stride, his garb, and the steady look of his eye which told of a growing confidence and competence. He looked like a horseman of the plains, fit for any emergency that might confront him.

Taken at a disadvantage by the suddenness of the meeting, Meldrum gave ground with a muttered oath. The young cattleman nodded to the trio and kept on his way. None of the others knew that his heart was hammering a tattoo against his ribs or that queer little chills chased each other down his spine.

Chet Fox ventured a sly dig at the ex-convict. "Looks a right healthy sick man, Dan."

"Who said he was sick?" growled Meldrum.

"Didn't you-all say he was good as dead?"

"A man can change his mind, Chet, can't he?" jeered Hart.

The blotched face of the bad man grew purple. "That'll be about enough from both of you. But I'll say this: When I get ready to settle with Mr. Beaudry you can order his coffin."

Nevertheless, Meldrum had the humiliating sense that he had failed to live up to his reputation as a killer. He had promised Battle Butte to give it something to talk about, but he had not meant to let the whisper pass that he was a four-flusher. His natural recourse was to further libations. These made for a sullen, ingrowing rage as the day grew older.

More than one well-meaning citizen carried to Roy the superfluous warning that Meldrum was in town and drinking hard. The young man thanked them quietly without comment. His reticence gave the impression of strength.

But Beaudry felt far from easy in mind. A good deal of water had flowed under the Big Creek bridge since the time when he had looked under the bed at nights for burglars. He had schooled himself not to yield to the impulses of his rabbit heart, but the unexpected clatter of hoofs still set his pulses aflutter. Why had fate snatched so gentle a youth from his law desk and flung him into such turbid waters to sink or swim? All he had asked was peace—friends, books, a quiet life. By some ironic quirk he found himself in scenes of battle and turmoil. As the son of John Beaudry he was expected to show an unflawed nerve, whereas his eager desire was to run away and hide.

He resisted the first panicky incitement to fly back to the Lazy Double D, and went doggedly about the business that had brought him to Battle Butte. Roy had come to meet a cattle-buyer from Denver and the man had wired that he would be in on the next train. Meanwhile Beaudry had to see the blacksmith, the feed-store manager, the station agent, and several others.

This kept him so busy that he reached the station only just in time to meet the incoming train. He introduced himself to the buyer, captured his suitcase, and turned to lead the way to the rig.

Meldrum lurched forward to intercept him. "Shus' a moment."

Roy went white. He knew the crisis was upon him. The right hand of the hillman was hidden under the breast of his coat. Even the cattle-buyer from Denver knew what was in that hand and edged toward the train. For this ruffian was plainly working himself into a rage sufficient to launch murder.

"Yore father railroaded me to the penitentiary—cooked up test'mony against me. You bust me with a club when I wasn't looking. Here's where I git even. See?"

The imminence of tragedy had swept the space about them empty of people. Roy knew with a sinking heart that it was between him and the hillman to settle this alone. He had been caught with the suitcase in his right hand, so that he was practically trapped unarmed. Before he could draw his revolver, Meldrum would be pumping lead.

Two months ago under similar circumstances terror had paralyzed Roy's thinking power. Now his brain functioned in spite of his fear. He was shaken to the center of his being, but he was not in panic. Immediately he set himself to play the poor cards he found in his hand.

"Liar!" Beaudry heard a chill voice say and knew it was his own. "Liar on both counts! My father sent you up because you were a thief. I beat your head off because you are a bully. Listen!" Roy shot the last word out in crescendo to forestall the result of a convulsive movement of the hand beneath his enemy's coat. "*Listen, if you want to live the day out,* you yellow coyote!"

Beaudry had scored his first point—to gain time for his argument to get home to the sodden brain. Dave Dingwell had told him that most men were afraid of something, though some hid it better than others; and he had added that Dan Meldrum had the murderer's dread lest vengeance overtake him unexpectedly. Roy knew now that his partner had spoken the true word. At that last stinging sentence, alarm had jumped to the blear eyes of the former convict.

"Whadjamean?" demanded Meldrum thickly, the menace of horrible things in his voice.

"Mean? Why, this. You came here to kill me, but you haven't the nerve to do it. You've reached the end of your rope, Dan Meldrum. You're a killer, but you'll never kill again. Murder me, and the law would hang you high as Haman—*if it ever got a chance.*"

The provisional clause came out with a little pause between each word to stress the meaning. The drunken man caught at it to spur his rage.

"Hmp! Mean you're man enough to beat the law to it?"

Beaudry managed to get out a derisive laugh. "Oh, no! Not when I have a suitcase in my right hand and you have the drop on me. I can't help myself—*and twenty men see it.*"

"Think they'll help you?" Meldrum swept his hand toward the frightened loungers and railroad officials. His revolver was out in the open now. He let its barrel waver in a semicircle of defiance.

"No. They won't help me, but they'll hang you. There's no hole where you can hide that they won't find you. Before night you'll be swinging underneath the big live-oak on the plaza. That's a prophecy for you to swallow, you four-flushing bully."

It went home like an arrow. The furtive eyes of the killer slid sideways to question this public which had scattered so promptly to save itself. Would the mob turn on him later and destroy him?

Young Beaudry's voice flowed on. "Even if you reached the hills, you would be doomed. Tighe can't save you—and he wouldn't try. Rutherford would wash his hands of you. They'll drag you back from your hole."

The prediction rang a bell in Meldrum's craven soul. Again he sought reassurance from those about him and found none. In their place he knew that he would revenge himself for present humiliation by cruelty later. He was checkmated.

It was an odd psychological effect of Beaudry's hollow defiance that confidence flowed in upon him as that of Meldrum ebbed. The chill drench of fear had lifted from his heart. It came to him that his enemy lacked the courage to kill. Safety lay in acting upon this assumption.

He raised his left hand and brushed the barrel of the revolver aside contemptuously, then turned and walked along the platform to the building. At the door he stopped, to lean faintly against the jamb, still without turning. Meldrum might shoot at any moment. It depended on how drunk he was, how clearly he could vision the future, how greatly his prophecy had impressed him. Cold chills ran up and down the spinal column of the young cattleman. His senses were reeling.

To cover his weakness Roy drew tobacco from his coat-pocket and rolled a cigarette with trembling fingers. He flashed a match. A moment later an insolent smoke wreath rose into the air and floated back toward Meldrum. Roy passed through the waiting-room to the street beyond.

Young Beaudry knew that the cigarette episode had been the weak bluff of one whose strength had suddenly deserted him. He had snatched at it to cover his weakness. But to the score or more who saw that spiral of smoke dissolving jauntily into air, no such thought was possible. The filmy wreath represented the acme of daredevil recklessness, the final proof of gameness in John Beaudry's son. He had turned his back on a drunken killer crazy for revenge and mocked the fellow at the risk of his life.

Presently Roy and the cattle-buyer were bowling down the street behind Dingwell's fast young four-year-olds. The Denver man did not know that his host was as weak from the reaction of the strain as a child stricken with fear.

CHAPTER 20

AT THE LAZY DOUBLE D

Dingwell squinted over the bunch of cattle in the corral. "Twenty dollars on the hoof, f.o.b. at the siding," he said evenly. "You to take the run of the pen, no culls."

"I heard you before," protested the buyer. "Learn a new song, Dingwell. I don't like the tune of that one. Make it eighteen and let me cull the bunch."

Dave garnered a straw clinging to the fence and chewed it meditatively. "Couldn't do it without hurting my conscience. Nineteen—no culls. That's my last word."

"I'd sure hate to injure your conscience, Dingwell," grinned the man from Denver. "Think I'll wait till you go to town and do business with your partner."

"Think he's easy, do you?"

"Easy!" the cattle-buyer turned the conversation to the subject uppermost in his mind. He had already decided to take the cattle and the formal agreement could wait. "Easy! Say, do you know what I saw that young man put over to-day at the depot?"

"I'll know when you've told me," suggested Dingwell.

The Denver man told his story and added editorial comment. "Gamest thing I ever saw in my life, by Jiminy—stood there with his back to the man-killer and lit a cigarette while the ruffian had his finger on the trigger of a six-gun ready to whang away at him. Can you beat that?"

The eyes of the cattleman gleamed, but his drawling voice was still casual. "Why didn't Meldrum shoot?"

"Triumph of mind over matter, I reckon. He *wanted* to shoot—was crazy to kill your friend. But—he didn't. Beaudry had talked him out of it."

"How?"

"Bullied him out of it—jeered at him and threatened

him and man-called him, with that big gun shining in his eyes every minute of the time."

Dingwell nodded slowly. He wanted to get the full flavor of this joyous episode that had occurred. "And the kid lit his cigarette while Meldrum, crazy as a hydrophobia skunk, had his gun trained on him?"

"That's right. Stood there with a kind o' you-be-damned placard stuck all over him, then got out the makin's and lit up. He tilted back that handsome head of his and blew a smoke wreath into the air. Looked like he'd plumb wiped Mr. Meldrum off his map. He's a world-beater, that young fellow is—doesn't know what fear is," concluded the buyer sagely.

"You don't say!" murmured Mr. Dingwell.

"Sure as you're a foot high. While I was trying to climb up the side of a railroad car to get out of range, that young guy was figuring it all out. He was explaining thorough to the bad man what would happen if he curled his forefinger another quarter of an inch. Just as cool and easy, you understand."

"You mean that he figured out his chances?"

"You bet you! He figured it all out, played a long shot, and won. The point is that it wouldn't help him any if this fellow Meldrum starred in a subsequent lynching. The man had been drinking like a blue blotter. Had he sense enough left to know his danger? Was his brain steady enough to hold him in check? Nobody could tell that. But your partner gambled on it and won."

This was meat and drink to Dave. He artfully pretended to make light of the whole affair in order to stir up the buyer to more details.

"I reckon maybe Meldrum was just bluffing. Maybe—"

"Bluffing!" The Coloradoan swelled. "Bluffing! I tell you there was murder in the fellow's eye. He had come there primed for a killing. If Beaudry had weakened by a hair's breadth, that forty-four would have pumped lead into his brain. Ask the train crew. Ask the station agent. Ask any one who was there."

"Maybeso," assented Dave dubiously. "But if he was so game, why didn't Beaudry go back and take Meldrum's gun from him?"

The buyer was on the spot with an eager, triumphant answer. "That just proves what I claim. He just brushed the fellow's gun aside and acted like he'd forgot the killer had a gun. 'Course, he could 'a' gone back and taken the gun. After what he'd already pulled off, that would have been like stealing apples from a blind Dutchman. But Beaudry wasn't going to give him that much consideration. Don't you see? Meldrum, or whatever his name is, was welcome to keep the revolver to play with. Your friend didn't care how many guns he was toting."

"I see. If he had taken the gun, Meldrum might have thought he was afraid of him."

"Now you're shouting. As it is the bad man is backed clear off the earth. It's like as if your partner said, 'Garnish yourself with forty-fours if you like, but don't get gay around me.' "

"So you think—"

"I think he's some bear-cat, that young fellow. When you're looking for something easy to mix with, go pick a grizzly or a wild cat, but don't you monkey with friend Beaudry. He's liable to interfere with your interior geography. . . . Say, Dingwell. Do I get to cull this bunch of longhorn skeletons you're misnaming cattle?"

"You do not."

The Denver man burlesqued a sigh. "Oh, well! I'll go broke dealing with you unsophisticated Shylocks of the range. The sooner the quicker. Send 'em down to the siding. I'll take the bunch."

Roy rode up on a pinto.

"Help! Help!" pleaded the Coloradoan of the young man.

"He means that I've unloaded this corral full of Texas dinosaurs on him at nineteen a throw," explained Dave.

"You've made a good bargain," Beaudry told the buyer.

" 'Course he has, and he knows it." Dingwell opened on Roy his gay smile. "I hear you've had a run-in with the bad man of Chicito Cañon, son."

Roy looked at the Denver man reproachfully. Ever since the affair on the station platform he had been flogging himself because he had driven away and left Meldrum in possession of the field. No doubt all Battle Butte knew now how frightened he had been. The women were gossiping about it over their tea, probably, and men were retailing the story in saloons and on sidewalks.

"I didn't want any trouble," he said apologetically. "I—I just left him."

"That's what I've been hearing," assented Dave dryly. "You merely showed him up for a false alarm and kicked him into the discard. That's good, and it's bad. We know

now that Meldrum won't fight you in the open. You've got him buffaloed. But he'll shoot you in the back if he can do it safely. I know the cur. After this don't ride alone, Roy, and don't ride that painted hoss at all. Get you a nice quiet buckskin that melts into the atmosphere like a patch of bunch grass. Them's my few well-chosen words of advice, as Mañana Bill used to say."

Three days later Beaudry, who had been superintending the extension of an irrigation ditch, rode up to the porch of the Lazy Double D ranch house and found Hal Rutherford, senior, with his chair tilted back against the wall. The smoke of his pipe mingled fraternally with that of Dingwell's cigar. He nodded genially to Roy without offering to shake hands.

"Mr. Rutherford dropped in to give us the latest about Meldrum," explained Dave. "Seems he had warned our friend the crook to lay off you, son. When Dan showed up again at the park, he bumped into Miss Beulah and said some pleasant things to her. He hadn't noticed that Jeff was just round the corner of the schoolhouse fixing up some dingus as a platform for the last day's speaking. Jeff always was hot-headed. Before he had got through with Mr. Meldrum, he had mussed his hair up considerable. Dan tried to gun him and got an awful walloping. He hit the trail to Jess Tighe's place. When Mr. Rutherford heard of it, he was annoyed. First off, because of what had happened at the depot. Second, and a heap more important, because the jailbird had threatened Miss Beulah. So he straddled a horse and called on Dan, who shook the dust of Huerfano Park from his bronco's hoofs *poco tiempo*."

"Where has he gone?" asked Roy.

"Nobody knows, and he won't tell. But, knowing Meldrum as we do, Rutherford and I have come to a coincidentical opinion, as you might say. He's a bad actor, that bird. We figure that he's waiting in the chaparral somewhere to pull off a revenge play, after which he means *pronto* to slide his freight across the line to the land of old Porf. Diaz."

"Revenge—on Jeff Rutherford—or who?"

"Son, that's a question. But Jeff won't be easily reached. On the whole, we think you're elected."

Roy's heart sank. If Meldrum had been kicked out of Huerfano Park, there was no room for him in New Mexico. Probably the fear of the Rutherfords had been a restraint upon him up to this time. But now that he had broken with them and was leaving the country, the man was free to follow the advice of Tighe. He was a bully whose prestige was tottering. It was almost sure that he would attempt some savage act of reprisal before he left. Beaudry had no doubt that he would be the victim of it.

"What am I to do, then?" he wanted to know, his voice quavering.

"Stay right here at the ranch. Don't travel from the house till we check up on Meldrum. Soon as he shows his hand, we'll jump him and run him out of the country. All you've got to do is to sit tight till we locate him."

"I'll not leave the house," Roy vowed fervently.

CHAPTER 21

ROY RIDES HIS PAINT HOSS

But he did.

For the next day Pat Ryan rode up to the Lazy Double D with a piece of news that took Roy straight to his pinto. Beulah Rutherford had disappeared. She had been out riding and Blacky had come home with an empty saddle. So far as was known, Brad Charlton had seen her last. He had met her just above the Laguna Sinks, had talked with her, and had left the young woman headed toward the mountains.

The word had reached Battle Butte through Slim Sanders, who had been sent down from Huerfano Park for help. The Rutherfords and their friends were already combing the hills for the lost girl, but the owner of the horse ranch wanted Sheriff Sweeney to send out posses as a border patrol. Opinion was divided. Some thought Beulah might have met a grizzly, been unhorsed, and fallen a victim to it. There was the possibility that she might have stumbled while climbing and hurt herself. According to Sanders, her father held to another view. He was convinced that Meldrum was at the bottom of the thing.

This was Roy's instant thought, too. He could not escape the sinister suggestion that through the girl the ruffian had punished them all. While he gave sharp, short orders to get together the riders of the ranch, his mind was busy with the situation. Had he better join Sweeney's posse and patrol the desert? Or would he help more by pushing straight into the hills?

Dingwell rode up and looked around in surprise. "What's the stir, son?"

His partner told him what he had heard and what he suspected.

Before he answered, Dave chewed a meditative cud. "Maybeso you're right—and maybe 'way off. Say you're wrong. Say Meldrum has nothing to do with this. In that case it is in the hills that we have got to find Miss Beulah."

"But he has. I feel sure he has. Mr. Ryan says Rutherford thinks so, too."

"Both you and Hal have got that crook Meldrum in yore minds. You've been thinking a lot about him, so you jump to the conclusion that what you're afraid of has happened. The chances are ten to one against it. But we'll say you're right. Put yourself in Meldrum's place. What would he do?"

Beaudry turned a gray, agonized face on his friend. "I don't know. What—what would he do?"

"The way to get at it is to figure yourself in his boots. Remember that you're a bad, rotten lot, cur to the bone. You meet up with this girl and get her in yore power. You've got a grudge against her because she spoiled yore plans, and because through her you were handed the whaling of yore life and are being hounded out of the country. You're sore clear through at all her people and at all her friends. Naturally, you're as sweet-tempered as a sore-headed bear, and you've probably been drinking like a sheepherder on a spree."

"I know what a devil he is. The question is how far

would he dare go?"

"You've put yore finger right on the point, son. What might restrain him wouldn't be any moral sense, but fear. He knows that once he touched Miss Rutherford, this country would treat him like a rattlesnake. He could not even be sure that the Rutherfords would not hunt him down in Mexico."

"You think he would let her alone, then?"

The old-timer shook his head. "No, he wouldn't do that. But I reckon he'd try to postpone a decision as long as he could. Unless he destroyed her in the first rush of rage, he wouldn't have the nerve to do it until he had made himself crazy drunk. It all depends on circumstances, but my judgment is—if he had a chance and if he didn't think it too great a risk—that he would try to hold her a prisoner as a sort of hostage to gloat over."

"You mean keep her—unharmed?"

They were already in the saddle and on the road. Dave looked across at his white-faced friend.

"I'm only guessing, Roy, but that's the way I figure it," he said gently.

"You don't think he would try to take her across the desert with him to Mexico."

Ryan shook his head.

"No chance. He couldn't make it. When he leaves the hills, Miss Rutherford will stay there."

"Alive?" asked Beaudry from a dry throat.

"Don't know."

"God!"

"So that whether Miss Beulah did or did not meet Meldrum, we have to look for her up among the mountains of the Big Creek watershed," concluded Dingwell. "I believe we'll find her safe and sound. Chances are Meldrum isn't within forty miles of her."

They were riding toward Lonesome Park, from which they intended to work up into the hills. Just before reaching the rim of the park, they circled around a young pine lying across the trail. Roy remembered the tree. It had stood on a little knoll, strong and graceful, reaching straight toward heaven with a kind of gallant uprightness. Now its trunk was snapped, its boughs crushed, its foliage turning sere. An envious wind had brought it low. Somehow that pine reminded Beaudry poignantly of the girl they were seeking. She, too, had always stood aloof, a fine and vital personality, before the eyes of men sufficient to herself. But as the evergreen had stretched its hundred arms toward light and sunshine, so Beulah Rutherford had cried dumbly to life for some vague good she could not formulate.

Were her pride and courage abased, too? Roy would not let himself believe it. The way of youth is to deny the truth of all signposts which point to the futility of beauty and strength. It would be a kind of apostasy to admit that her sweet, lissom grace might be forever crushed and bruised.

They rode hard and steadily. Before dusk they were well up toward the divide among the wooded pockets of the hills. From one of these a man came to meet them.

"It's Hal Rutherford," announced Ryan, who was riding in front with Dingwell.

The owner of the horse ranch nodded a greeting as he drew up in front of them. He was unshaven and gaunt.

Furrows of anxiety lined his face.

"Anything new, Hal?" asked Dave.

"Not a thing. We're combing the hills thorough."

"You don't reckon that maybe a cougar—?" Ryan stopped. It occurred to him that his suggestion was not a very cheerful one.

Rutherford looked at the little Irishman from bleak eyes. The misery in them was for the moment submerged in a swift tide of hate. "A two-legged cougar, Pat. If I meet up with him, I'll take his hide off inch by inch."

"Meaning Meldrum?" asked Roy.

"Meaning Meldrum." A spasm of pain shot across the face of the man. "If he's done my little girl any meanness, he'd better blow his head off before I get to him."

"Don't believe he'd dare hurt Miss Beulah, Rutherford. Meldrum belongs to the coyote branch of the wolf family. I've noticed it's his night to howl only when hunters are liable to be abed. If he's in this thing at all, I'll bet he's trying to play both ends against the middle. We'll sure give him a run for his white alley," Dingwell concluded.

"Hope you're right, Dave," Rutherford added in a voice rough with the feeling he could not suppress: "I appreciate it that you boys from the Lazy Double D came after what has taken place."

Dave grinned cheerfully. "Sho, Hal! Maybe Beaudry and I aren't sending any loving-cups up to you and yours, but we don't pull any of that sulk-in-the-tent stuff when our good friend Beulah Rutherford is lost in the hills. She went through for us proper, and we ain't going to quit till we bring her back to you as peart and sassy as that calf there."

"What part of the country do you want us to work?" asked Ryan.

"You can take Del Oro and Lame Cow Creeks from the divide down to the foothills," Rutherford answered. "I'll send one of the boys over to boss the round-up. He'll know the ground better than you lads. Make camp here to-night and he'll join you before you start. To-morrow evening I'll have a messenger meet you on the flats. We're trying to keep in touch with each other, you understand."

Rutherford left them making camp. They were so far up in the mountains that the night was cool, even though the season was midsummer. Unused to sleeping out-doors as yet, Roy lay awake far into the night. His nerves were jumpy. The noises of the grazing horses and of the four-footed inhabitants of the night startled him more than once from a cat-nap. His thoughts were full of Beulah Rutherford. Was she alive or dead to-night, in peril or in safety?

At last, in the fag end of the night, he fell into sound sleep that was untroubled. From this he was wakened in the first dim dawn by the sound of his companions stir-ring. A fire was already blazing and breakfast in process of making. He rose and stretched his stiff limbs. Every bone seemed to ache from contact with the hard ground.

While they were eating breakfast, a man rode up and dismounted. A long, fresh zigzag scar stretched across his forehead. It was as plain to be seen as the scowl which drew his heavy eyebrows together.

“ ’Lo, Charlton. Come to boss this round-up for us?” asked Dingwell cheerily.

The young man nodded sulkily. “Hal sent me. The boys weren’t with him.” He looked across the fire at Beaudry, and there was smouldering rage in his narrowed eyes.

Roy murmured “Good-morning” in a rather stifled voice. This was the first time he had met Charlton since they had clashed in the arcade of the Silver Dollar. That long deep scar fascinated him. He felt an impulse to apologize humbly for having hit him so hard. To put such a mark on a man for life was a liberty that might well be taken as a personal affront. No wonder Charlton hated him—and as their eyes met now, Roy had no doubt about that. The man was his enemy. Some day he would even the score. Again Beaudry’s heart felt the familiar drench of an icy wave.

Charlton did not answer his greeting. He flushed to his throat, turned abruptly on his heel, and began to talk with Ryan. The hillman wanted it clearly understood that the feud he cherished was only temporarily abandoned. But even Roy noticed that the young Admirable Crichton had lost some of his debonair aplomb.

The little Irishman explained this with a grin to Dave as they were riding together half an hour later. “It’s not so easy to get away with that slow insolence of his while he’s wearing that forgit-me-not young Beaudry handed him in the mix-up.”

“Sort of spoils the toutensemble, as that young Melrose tenderfoot used to say—kinder as if a bald-haided guy was playing Romeo and had lost his wig in the shuffle," agreed Dave.

By the middle of the forenoon they were well up in the headwaters of the two creeks they were to work. Charlton divided the party so as to cover both watersheds as they swept slowly down. Roy was on the extreme right of those working Del Oro.

It was a rough country, with wooded draws cached in unexpected pockets of the hills. Here a man might lie safely on one of a hundred ledges while the pursuit drove past within fifty feet of him. As Roy's pinto clambered up and down the steep hills, he recalled the advice of Dave to ride a buckskin "that melts into the atmosphere like a patch of bunch grass." He wished he had taken that advice. A man looking for revenge could crouch in the chaparral and with a crook of his finger send winged death at his enemy. A twig crackling under the hoof of his horse more than once sent an electric shock through his pulses. The crash of a bear through the brush seemed to stop the beating of his heart.

Charlton had made a mistake in putting Beaudry on the extreme right of the drive. The number of men combing the two creeks was not enough to permit close contact. Sometimes a rider was within hail of his neighbor. More often he was not. Roy, unused to following the rodeo, was deflected by the topography of the ridge so far to the right that he lost touch with the rest.

By the middle of the afternoon he had to confess to himself with chagrin that he did not even know how to reach Del Oro. While he had been riding the rough wooded ridge above, the creek had probably made a sharp turn to the left. Must he go back the way he had come? Or could he cut across country to it? It was humiliating that he could not even follow a small river without losing the stream and himself. He could vision the cold sneer of Charlton when he failed to appear at the night rendezvous. Even his friends would be annoyed at such helplessness.

After an hour's vain search he was more deeply tangled in the web of hills. He was no longer even sure how to get down from them into the lower reaches of country toward which he was aiming.

While he hesitated on a ridge there came to him a faint, far cry. He gave a shout of relief, then listened for his answer. It did not come. He called again, a third time, and a fourth. The wind brought back no reply. Roy rode in the direction of the sound that had first registered itself on his ears, stopping every minute or two to shout. Once he fancied he heard again the voice.

Then, unexpectedly, the cry came perfectly clear, over to the right scarcely a hundred yards. A little arroyo of quaking aspens lay between him and the one who called. He dismounted, tied his horse to a sapling, and pushed through the growth of young trees. Emerging from these, he climbed the brow of the hill and looked around. Nobody was in sight.

"Where are you?" he shouted.

"Here—in the prospect hole."

His pulses crashed. That voice—he would have known it out of a million.

A small dirt dump on the hillside caught his eye. He ran forward to the edge of a pit and looked down.

The haggard eyes of Beulah Rutherford were lifted to meet his.

CHAPTER 22

MISS RUTHERFORD SPEAKS HER MIND

For the first time in over a year an itinerant preacher was to hold services in the Huerfano Park schoolhouse. He would speak, Beulah Rutherford knew, to a mere handful of people, and it was to mitigate his disappointment that she rode out into the hills on the morning of her disappearance to find an armful of columbines for decorating the desk-pulpit. The man had written Miss Rutherford and asked her to notify the community. She had seen that the news was carried to the remotest ranch, but she expected for a congregation only a scatter of patient women and restless children with three or four coffee-brown youths in high-heeled boots on the back row to represent the sinners.

It was a brave, clean world into which she rode this summer morning. The breeze brought to her nostrils the sweet aroma of the sage. Before her lifted the saw-toothed range into a sky of blue sprinkled here and there with light mackerel clouds. Blacky pranced with fire and intelligence, eager to reach out and leave behind him the sunny miles.

Near the upper end of the park she swung up an arroyo that led to Big Flat Top. A drawling voice stopped her.

"Oh, you, Beulah Rutherford! Where away this glad mo'ning?"

A loose-seated rider was lounging in the saddle on a little bluff fifty yards away. His smile reminded her of a new copper kettle shining in the sun.

"To find columbines for church decorations," she said with an answering smile.

"Have you been building a church since I last met up with you?"

"There will be services in the schoolhouse to-morrow at three P.M., conducted by the Reverend Melancthon Smith. Mr. Charlton is especially invited to attend."

"Maybe I'll be there. You can't sometimes 'most always tell. I'm going to prove I've got nothing against religion by going with you to help gather the pulpit decorations."

"That's very self-sacrificing of you." She flashed a look of gay derision at him as he joined her. "Sure you can afford to waste so much time?"

"I don't call it wasted. But since you've invited me so hearty to your picnic, I'd like to be sure you've got grub enough in the chuck wagon for two," he said with a glance at her saddlebags.

"I'm not sure. Maybe you had better not come."

"Oh, I'm coming if you starve me. Say, Beulah, have you heard about Jess Tighe?"

"What about him?"

"He had a stroke last night. Doc Spindler thinks he won't live more than a few hours."

Beulah mused over that for a few moments without answer. She had no liking for the man, but it is the way of youth to be shocked at the approach of death. Yet she knew this would help to clear up the situation. With the evil influence of Tighe removed, there would be a chance for the park to develop along more wholesome lines. He had been like a sinister shadow that keeps away the sunlight.

She drew a deep breath. "I don't wish him any harm. But it will be a good thing for all of us when he can't make us more sorrow and trouble."

"He never made me any," Charlton answered.

"Didn't he?" She looked steadily across at him. "You can't tell me he didn't plan that express robbery, for instance."

"Meaning that I was in the party that pulled it off?" he asked, flushing.

"I know well enough you were in it—knew it all along. It's the sort of thing you couldn't keep out of."

"How about Ned? Do you reckon he could keep out of it?" She detected rising anger beneath his controlled voice.

"Not with you leading him on." Her eyes poured scorn on him. "And I'm sure he would appreciate your loyalty in telling me he was in it."

"Why do you jump on me, then?" he demanded sulkily. "And I didn't say Ned was in that hold-up—any more than I admit having been in it myself. Are you trying to make trouble with me? Is that it?"

"I don't care whether I make trouble with you or not. I'm not going to pretend and make-believe, if that's what you want. I don't have to do it."

"I see you don't," he retorted bluntly. "I suppose you don't have to mind your own business either."

"It is my business when Ned follows you into robbery."

"Maybe I followed him," he jeered.

She bit back the tart answer on her tongue. What was the use of quarreling? It used to be that they were good friends, but of late they jangled whenever they met. Ever since the Western Express affair she had held a grudge at him. Six months ago she had almost promised to marry him. Now nothing was farther from her thoughts.

But he was still very much of the mind that she should.

"What's the matter with you, Boots?" he wanted to know roughly. "You used to have some sense. You weren't always flying out at a fellow. Now there's no way of pleasing you."

"I suppose it is odd that I don't want my friends to be thieves," she flung out bitterly.

"Don't use that word if you mean me," he ordered.

"What word shall I substitute?"

He barely suppressed an oath. "I know what's ailing you. We're not smooth enough up here for you. We're not educated up to your standard. If I'd been to Cornell, say—"

"Take care," she warned with a flash of anger in her black eyes.

"Oh, I don't know. Why should I cull my words so careful? I notice yours ain't handpicked. Ever since this guy Beaudry came spying into the park, you've had no use for me. You have been throwing yourself at his head and couldn't see any one else."

She gasped. "How dare you, Brad Charlton?"

His jealousy swept away the prudence that had dammed his anger. "Didn't you take him out driving? Didn't you spend a night alone with him and Dave

Dingwell? Didn't you hotfoot it down to Hart's because you was afraid yore precious spy would meet up with what he deserved?"

Beulah drew up Blacky abruptly. "Now you can leave me. Don't stop to say good-bye. I hate you. I don't ever want to see you again."

He had gone too far and he knew it. Sulkily he began to make his apology. "You know how fond I am of you, Boots. You know—"

"Yes, I ought to. I've heard it often enough," she interrupted curtly. "That's probably why you insult me?"

Her gypsy eyes stabbed him. She was furiously angry. He attempted to explain. "Now, listen here, Beulah. Let's be reasonable."

"Are you going up or down?" she demanded. "I'm going the other way. Take one road or the other, you—you scandal-monger."

Never a patient man, he too gave rein to his anger. "Since you want to know, I'm going down—to Battle Butte, where I'll likely meet yore friend Beaudry and settle an account or two with him. I reckon before I git through with him he'll yell something besides Cornell."

The girl laughed scornfully. "Last time I saw him he had just beaten a dozen or so of you. How many friends are you going to take along this trip?"

Already her horse was taking the trail. She called the insult down to him over her shoulder.

But before she had gone a half-mile her eyes were blind with tears. Why did she get so angry? Why did she say such things? Other girls were ladylike and soft-spoken. Was there a streak of commonness in her that made possible such a scene as she had just gone through? In her heart she longed to be a lady—gentle, refined, sweet of spirit. Instead of which she was a bad-tempered tomboy. “Miss Spitfire” her brothers sometimes called her, and she knew the name was justified.

Take this quarrel now with Brad. She had had no intention of breaking with him in that fashion. Why couldn’t she dismiss a lover as girls in books do, in such a way as to keep him for a friend? She had not meant, anyhow, to bring the matter to issue to-day. One moment they had been apparently the best of comrades. The next they had been saying hateful things to each other. What he had said was unforgivable, but she had begun by accusing him of complicity in the train robbery. Knowing how arrogant he was, she might have guessed how angry criticism would make him.

Yet she was conscious of a relief that it was over with at last. Charlton was proud. He would leave her alone unless she called him to her side. Her tears were for the humiliating way in which they had wrenched apart rather than for the fact of the break.

She knew his temper. Nothing on earth could keep him from flying at the throat of Roy Beaudry now. Well, she had no interest in either of them, she reminded herself impatiently. It was none of her business how they settled their differences. Yet, as Blacky followed the stiff trail to Big Flat Top, her mind was wretchedly troubled.

Beulah had expected to find her columbines in a gulch back of Big Flat Top, but the flowers were just past their prime here. The petals fell fluttering at her touch. She hesitated. Of course, she did not have to get columbines for the preaching service. Sweet-peas would do very well. But she was a young woman who did not like to be beaten. She had plenty of time, and she wanted an excuse to be alone all day. Why not ride over to Del Oro Creek, where the season was later and the columbines would be just coming on?

The ayes had it, and presently Miss Rutherford was winding deeper into the great hills that skirted Flat Top. Far in the gulches, dammed by the small thick timber, she came on patches of snow upon which the sun never shone. Once a ptarmigan started from the brush at her feet. An elk sprang up from behind a log, stared at her, and crashed away through the fallen timber.

Her devious road took Beulah past a hill flaming with goldenrod and Indian paintbrushes. A wealth of color decorated every draw, for up here at the roots of the peaks blossoms rioted in great splashes that ran to the snowbanks.

After all, she had to go lower for her favorite blooms. On Del Oro she found columbines, but in no great profusion. She wandered from the stream, leading Blacky by the bridle. On a hillside just above an aspen grove the girl came upon scattered clumps of them. Tying the pony loosely to a clump of bushes, she began to gather the delicate blue wild flowers.

The blossoms enticed her feet to the edge of a prospect hole long since abandoned. A clump of them grew from the side of the pit about a foot below the level of the ground. Beulah reached for them, and at the same moment the ground caved beneath her feet. She clutched at a bush in vain as she plunged down.

Jarred by the fall, Beulah lay for a minute in a huddle at the bottom of the pit. She was not quite sure that no bones were broken. Before she had time to make certain, a sound brought her rigidly to her feet. It was a light loose sound like the shaking of dried peas in their pods. No dweller of the outdoors Southwest could have failed to recognize it, and none but would have been startled by it.

The girl whipped her revolver from its scabbard and stood pressed against the rock wall while her eyes searched swiftly the prison into which she had fallen. Again came that light swift rattle with its sinister menace.

The enemy lay coiled across the pit from her, head and neck raised, tongue vibrating. Beulah fired—once—twice—a third time. It was enough. The rattlesnake ceased writhing.

The first thing she did was to examine every inch of her prison to make sure there were no more rattlers. Satisfied as to this, she leaned faintly against the wall. The experience had been a shock even to her sound young nerves.

CHAPTER 23

IN THE PIT

Beulah shut her eyes to steady herself. From the impact of her fall she was still shaken. Moreover, though she had shot many a rattlesnake, this was the first time she had ever been flung head first into the den of one. It would have been easy to faint, but she denied herself the luxury of it and resolutely fought back the swimming lightness in her head.

Presently she began to take stock of her situation. The prospect hole was circular in form, about ten feet across and nine feet deep. The walls were of rock and smooth clay. Whatever timbering had been left by the prospector was rotted beyond use. It crumbled at the weight of her foot.

How was she to get out? Of course, she would find some way, she told herself. But how? Blacky was tied to a bush not fifty yards away, and fastened to the saddle horn was the rope that would have solved her problem quickly enough. If she had it here— But it might as well be at Cheyenne for all the good it would do her now.

Perhaps she could dig footholds in the wall by means of which she could climb out. Unbuckling the spur from her heel, she used the rowel as a knife to jab a hole in the clay. After half an hour of persistent work she looked at the result in dismay. She had gouged a hollow, but it was not one where her foot could rest while she made steps above.

Every few minutes Beulah stopped work to shout for help. It was not likely that anybody would be passing. Probably she had been the only person on this hill for months. But she dared not miss any chance.

For it was coming home to her that she might die of starvation in this prison long before her people found the place. By morning search-parties would be out over the hills looking for her. But who would think to find her away over on Del Oro? If Brad had carried out his threat immediately and gone down to Battle Butte, nobody would know even the general direction in which to seek.

With every hour Beulah grew more troubled. Late in the afternoon she fired a fourth shot from her revolver in the hope that some one might hear the sound and investigate. The sun set early for her. She watched its rays climb the wall of her prison while she worked half-heartedly with the spur. After a time the light began to fade, darkness swept over the land, and she had to keep moving in order not to chill.

Never had she known such a night. It seemed to the tortured girl that morning would never come. She counted the stars above her. Sometimes there were more. Sometimes fewer. After an eternity they began to fade out in the sky. Day was at hand.

She fired the fifth shot from her revolver. Her voice was hoarse from shouting, but she called every few minutes. Then, when she was at the low ebb of hope, there came an answer to her call. She fired her last shot. She called and shouted again and again. The voice that came back to her was close at hand.

"I'm down in the prospect hole," she cried.

Another moment, and she was looking up into the face of a man, Dan Meldrum. In vacant astonishment he gazed down at her.

"Whad you doing here?" he asked roughly.

"I fell in. I've been here all night." Her voice broke a little. "Oh, I'm so glad you've come."

It was of no importance that he was a man she detested, one who had quarreled with her father and been thrashed by her brother for insulting her. All she thought of was that help had come to her at last and she was now safe.

He stared down at her with a kind of drunken malevolence.

"So you fell in, eh?"

"Yes. Please help me out right away. My riata is tied to Blacky's saddle."

He looked around. "Where?"

"Isn't Blacky there? He must have broken loose, then. Never mind. Pass me down the end of a young sapling and you can pull me up."

"Can I?"

For the first time she felt a shock of alarm. There was in his voice something that chilled her, something inexpressibly cruel.

"I'll see my father rewards you. I'll see you get well paid," she promised, and the inflection of the words was an entreaty.

"You will, eh?"

"Anything you want," she hurried on. "Name it. If we can give it to you, I promise it."

His drunken brain was functioning slowly. This was the girl who had betrayed him up in Chicito Cañon, the one who had frustrated his revenge at Hart's. On account of her young Rutherford had given him the beating of his life and Hal had driven him from Huerfano Park. First and last she was the rock upon which his fortunes had split. Now chance had delivered her into his hands. What should he do with her? How could he safely make the most of the opportunity?

It did not for an instant occur to him to haul her from the pit and send her rejoicing on the homeward way. He intended to make her pay in full. But how? How get his revenge and not jeopardize his own safety?

"Won't you hurry, please?" she pleaded. "I'm hungry—and thirsty. I've been here all night and most of yesterday. It's been . . . rather awful."

He rubbed his rough, unshaven cheek while his little pig eyes looked down into hers. "Tha' so? Well, I dunno as it's any business of mine where you spend the night or how long you stay there. I had it put up to me to lay off 'n interfering with you. Seems like yore family got notions I was insulting you. That young bully Jeff jumped me whilst I wasn't looking and beat me up. Hal Rutherford ordered me to pull my freight. That's all right. I won't interfere in what don't concern me. Yore family says 'Hands off!' Fine. Suits me. Stay there or get out. It's none of my business. See?"

"You don't mean you'll . . . leave me here?" she cried in horror.

"Sure," he exulted. "If I pulled you out of there, like as not you'd have me beat up again. None o' my business! That's what yore folks have been drilling into me. I reckon they're right. Anyhow, I'll play it safe."

"But— Oh, you can't do that. Even you can't do such a thing," she cried desperately. "Why, men don't do things like that."

"Don't they? Watch me, missie." He leaned over the pit, his broken, tobacco-stained teeth showing in an evil grin. "Just keep an eye on yore Uncle Dan. Nobody ever yet done me a meanness and got away with it. I reckon the Rutherfords won't be the first. It ain't on the cyards," he boasted.

"You're going away . . . to leave me here . . . to starve?"

"Who said anything about going away? I'll stick around for a while. It's none of my business whether you starve or live high. Do just as you please about that. I'll let you alone, like I promised Jeff I would. You Rutherfords have got no call to object to being starved, anyhow. *Whad you do to Dave Dingwell in Chicito?*"

After all, she was only a girl in spite of her little feminine ferocities and her pride and her gameness. She had passed through a terrible experience, had come out of it to apparent safety and had been thrown back into despair. It was natural that sobs should shake her slender body as she leaned against the quartz wall of her prison and buried her head in her forearm.

When presently the sobs grew fewer and less violent, Beulah became aware without looking up that her tormentor had taken away his malignant presence. This was at first a relief, but as the hours passed an acute fear seized her. Had he left her alone to die? In spite of her knowledge of the man, she had clung to the hope that he would relent. But if he had gone—

She began again to call at short intervals for help. Sometimes tears of self-pity choked her voice. More than once she beat her brown fists against the rock in an ecstasy of terror.

Then again he was looking down at her, a hulk of venom, eyes bleared with the liquor he had been drinking.

"Were you calling me, missie?" he jeered.

"Let me out," she demanded. "When my brothers find me—"

"If they find you," he corrected with a hiccough.

"They'll find me. By this time everybody in Huerfano Park is searching for me. Before night half of Battle Butte will be in the saddle. Well, when they find me, do you think you won't be punished for this?"

"For what?" demanded the man. "You fell in. I haven't touched you."

"Will that help you, do you think?"

His rage broke into speech. "You're aimin' to stop my clock, are you? Take another guess, you mischief-making vixen. What's to prevent me from emptying my forty-four into you when I get good and ready, then hitting the trail for Mexico?"

She knew he was speaking the thoughts that had been drifting through his mind in whiskey-lit ruminations. That he was a wanton killer she had always heard. If he could persuade himself it could be done with safety, he would not hesitate to make an end of her.

This was the sort of danger she could fight against—and she did.

"I'll tell you what's to prevent you," she flung back, as it were in a kind of careless scorn. "Your fondness for your worthless hide. If they find me shot to death, they will know who did it. You couldn't hide deep enough in Chihuahua to escape them. My father would never rest till he had made an end of you."

Her argument sounded appallingly reasonable to him. He knew the Rutherfords. They would make him pay his debt to them with usury.

To stimulate his mind he took another drink, after which he stared down at her a long time in sullen, sulky silence. She managed at the same time to irritate him and tempt him and fill his coward heart with fear of consequences. Through the back of his brain from the first there had been filtering thoughts that were like crouching demons. They reached toward her and drew back in alarm. He was too white-livered to go through with his villainy boldly.

He recorked the bottle and put it in his hip pocket. " 'Nough said," he blustered. "Me, I'll git on my hawss and be joggin' along to Mex. I'll take chances on their finding you before you're starved. After that it won't matter to me when they light on yore body."

"Oh, yes, it will," she corrected him promptly. "I'm going to write a note and tell just what has happened. It will be found beside me in case they . . . don't reach here in time."

The veins in his blotched face stood out as he glared down at her while he adjusted himself to this latest threat. Here, too, she had him. He had gone too far. Dead or alive, she was a menace to his safety.

Since he must take a chance, why not take a bigger one, why not follow the instigation of the little crouching devils in his brain? He leered down at her with what was meant to be an ingratiating smile.

"Sho! What's the use of we 'uns quarreling, Miss Beulah? I ain't got nothing against you. Old Dan he always liked you fine. I reckon you didn't know that, did you?"

Her quick glance was in time to catch his face napping. The keen eyes of the girl pounced on his and dragged from them a glimpse of the depraved soul of the ruffian.

Silently and warily she watched him.

"I done had my little joke, my dear," he went on. "Now we'll be heap good friends. Old Dan ain't such a bad sort. There's lots of folks worse than Dan. That's right. Now, what was that you said a while ago about giving me anything I wanted?"

"I said my father would pay you anything in reason." Her throat was parched, but her eyes were hard and bright. No lithe young panther of the forest could have been more alert than she.

"Leave yore dad out of it. He ain't here, and, anyway, I ain't having any truck with him. Just say the word, Miss Beulah, and I'll git a pole and haul you up in a jiffy."

Beulah made a mistake. She should have waited till she was out of the pit before she faced the new issue. But her horror of the man was overpowering. She unscabbarded swiftly the revolver at her side and lifted it defiantly toward him.

"I'll stay here."

Again he foamed into rage. The girl had stalemated him once more. "Then stay, you little wild cat. You've had yore chance. I'm through with you." He bared his teeth in a snarling grin and turned his back on her.

Beulah heard him slouching away. Presently there came the sound of a furiously galloping horse. The drumming of the hoofbeats died in the distance.

During the rest of the day she saw no more of the man. It swept over her toward evening in a wave of despair that he had left her to her fate.

CHAPTER 24

THE BAD MAN DECIDES NOT TO SHOOT

Beulah woke from a sleep of exhaustion to a world into which the morning light was just beginning to sift. The cold had penetrated to her bones. She was stiff and cramped and sore from the pressure of the rock bed against her tender young flesh. For nearly two days she had been without food or drink. The urge of life in her was at low tide.

But the traditions among which she had been brought up made pluck a paramount virtue. She pushed from her the desire to weep in self-pity over her lot. Though her throat was raw and swollen, she called at regular intervals during the morning hours while the sun climbed into view of her ten-foot beat. Even when it rode the heavens a red-hot cannon ball directly above her, the hoarse and lonely cry of the girl echoed back from the hillside every few minutes. There were times when she wanted to throw herself down and give up to despair, but she knew there would be opportunity for that when she could no longer fight for her life. The shadow was beginning to climb the eastern wall of the pit before Beaudry's shout reached her ears faintly. Her first thought was that she must already be delirious. Not till she saw him at the edge of the prospect hole was she sure that her rescuer was a reality.

At the first sight of her Roy wanted to trumpet to high heaven the joy that flooded his heart. He had found her—alive. After the torment of the night and the worry of the day he had come straight to her in his wandering, and he had reached her in time.

But when he saw her condition pity welled up in him. Dark hollows had etched themselves into her cheeks. Tears swam in her eyes. Her lips trembled weakly from emotion. She leaned against the side of the pit to support herself on account of the sudden faintness that engulfed her senses. He knelt and stretched his hands toward her, but the pit was too deep.

"You'll have to get a pole or a rope," she told him quietly.

Beaudry found the dead trunk of a young sapling and drew the girl up hand over hand. On the brink she stumbled and he caught her in his arms to save her from falling back into the prospect hole.

For a moment she lay close to him, heart beating against heart. Then, with a little sobbing sigh, she relaxed and began to weep. Her tears tugged at his sympathy, but none the less the pulses pounded in his veins. He held her tight, with a kind of savage tenderness, while his body throbbed with the joy of her. She had come to him with the same sure instinct that brings a child to its mother's arms. All her pride and disdain and suspicion had melted like summer mists in her need of the love and comfort he could give her.

"It's all right now. You're safe. Nothing can hurt you," he promised.

"I know, but you don't know—what—what—" She broke off, shuddering.

Still with his arm about her, he led Beulah to his horse. Here he made her sit down while he gave her water and food. Bit by bit she told him the story of her experience. He suffered poignantly with her, but he could not be grateful enough that the finger-tip of destiny had pointed him to her prison. He thanked his rather vague gods that it had been his footsteps rather than those of another man that had wandered here to save her.

What surprised and wholly delighted him was the feminine quality of her. He had thought of her before as a wild young creature full of pride and scorn and anger, but with a fine barbaric loyalty that might yet redeem her from her faults. He had never met a young woman so hard, so self-reliant. She had asked no odds because of her sex. Now all this harshness had melted. No strange child could have been more shy and gentle. She had put herself into his hands and seemed to trust him utterly. His casual opinions were accepted by her as if they had been judgments of Solomon.

Roy spread his blankets and put the saddle-bags down for a pillow.

"We're not going to stay here to-night, are we?" she asked, surprised.

He smiled. "No, you're going to lie down and sleep for an hour. When you wake, supper will be ready. You're all in now, but with a little rest you will be fit to travel."

"You won't go away while I sleep?" she said.

"Do you think it likely? No, you can't get rid of me that easy. I'm a regular adhesive plaster for sticking."

"I don't want to get rid of you," she answered naïvely. "I'd be afraid without you. Will you promise to stay close all the time I sleep?"

"Yes."

"I know I won't sleep, but if you want me to try—"

"I do."

She snuggled down into the blankets and was asleep in five minutes.

Beaudry watched her with hungry eyes. What was the use of denying to himself that he loved her? If he had not known it before, the past half-hour had made it clear to him. With those wan shadows below her long eye-lashes and that charming manner of shy dependence upon him, she was infinitely more attractive to him than she had ever been before.

Beulah Rutherford was not the kind of girl he had thought of as a sweetheart in his daydreams. His fancies had hovered hazily about some imaginary college girl, one skilled in the finesse of the rules that society teaches young women in self-defense. Instead, he had fallen in love with a girl who could not play the social game at all. She was almost the only one he had known who never used any perfume; yet her atmosphere was fragrant as one of the young pines in her own mountain park. The young school-teacher was vital, passionate, and—he suspected, fiercely tender. For her lover there would be rare gifts in her eyes, wonderful largesse in her smile. The man who could qualify as her husband must be clean and four-square and game from the soles of his feet up—such a man as Dave Dingwell, except that the cattleman was ten years too old for her.

Her husband! What was he thinking about? Roy brought his bolting thoughts up with a round turn. There could be no question of marriage between her father's daughter and his father's son. Hal Rutherford had put that out of doubt on the day when he had ridden to the Elephant Corral to murder Sheriff Beaudry. No decent man could marry the daughter of the man who had killed his father in cold blood. Out of such a wedding could come only sorrow and tragedy.

And if this were not bar enough between them, there was another. Beulah Rutherford could never marry a man who was a physical coward. It was a dear joy to his soul that she had broken down and wept and clung to him. But this was the sex privilege of even a brave woman. A man had to face danger with a nerve of tested iron, and that was a thing he could never do.

Roy was stretched on the moss face down, his chin resting on the two cupped palms of his hands. Suddenly he sat up, every nerve tense and alert. Silently he got to his feet and stole down into the aspen grove. With great caution he worked his way into the grove and peered through to the hillside beyond. A man was standing by the edge of the prospect hole. He was looking down into it. Young Beaudry recognized the heavy, slouched figure at the first glance.

Not for an instant did he hesitate about what he meant to do. The hour had come when he and Dan Meldrum must have an accounting. From its holster he drew his revolver and crept forward toward the bad man. His eyes were cold and hard as chilled steel. He moved with the long, soft stride of a panther crouched for the kill. Not till the whole thing was over did he remember that for once the ghost of fear had been driven from his soul. He thought only of the wrongs of Beulah Rutherford, the girl who had fallen asleep in the absolute trust that he would guard her from all danger. This scoundrel had given her two days of living hell. Roy swore to pay the fellow in full.

Meldrum turned. He recognized Beaudry with a snarl of rage and terror. Except one of the Rutherfords there was no man on earth he less wanted to meet. The forty-four in his hand jerked up convulsively. The miscreant was in two minds whether to let fly or wait.

Roy did not even falter in his stride. He did not raise the weapon in his loosely hanging hand. His eyes bored as steadily as gimlets into the craven heart of the outlaw.

Meldrum, in a panic, warned him back. His nerve was gone. For two days he had been drinking hard, but the liquor had given out at midnight. He needed a bracer badly. This was no time for him to go through with a finish fight against such a man as Beaudry.

"Keep yore distance and tell me what you want," the ex-convict repeated hoarsely. "If you don't, I'll gun you sure."

The young cattleman stopped about five yards from him. He knew exactly what terms he meant to give the enemy.

"Put your gun up," he ordered sharply.

"Who's with you?"

"Never mind who is with me. I can play this hand alone. Put up that gun and then we'll talk."

That suited Meldrum. If it was a question of explanations, perhaps he could whine his way out of this. What he had been afraid of was immediate battle. One cannot talk bullets aside.

Slowly he pushed his revolver into its holster, but the

hand of the man rested still on the butt.

"I came back to help Miss Rutherford out of this prospect hole," he whimperingly complained. "When onc't I got sober, I done recalled that she was here. So I hit the trail back."

Meldrum spoke the exact truth. When the liquor was out of him, he became frightened at what he had done. He had visions of New Mexico hunting him down like a wild dog. At last, unable to stand it any longer, he had come back to free her.

"That's good. Saves me the trouble of looking for you. I'm going to give you a choice. You and I can settle this thing with guns right here and now. That's one way out for you. I'll kill you where you stand."

"W—what's the other way?" stammered the outlaw.

"The other way is for you to jump into that prospect hole. I'll ride away and leave you there to starve."

"Goddlemighty! You wouldn't do that," Meldrum wheedled. "I didn't go for to hurt Miss Rutherford any. Didn't I tell you I was drunk?"

"Dead or alive, you're going into that prospect hole. Make up your mind to that."

The bad man moistened his dry lips with the tip of his tongue. He stole one furtive glance around. Could he gun this man and make his getaway?

"Are any of the Rutherfords back of that clump of aspens?" he asked in a hoarse whisper.

"Yes."

"Do . . . do they know I'm here?"

"Not yet."

Tiny beads of sweat stood out on the blotched face of

the rustler. He was trapped. Even if he fired through the leather holster and killed Beaudry, there would be no escape for him on his tired horse.

"Gimme a chanc't," he pleaded desperately. "Honest to God, I'll clear out of the country for good. I'll quit helling around and live decent. I'll—"

"You'll go into the pit."

Meldrum knew as he looked into that white, set face that he had come to his day of judgment. But he mumbled a last appeal.

"I'm an old man, Mr. Beaudry. I ain't got many years—"

"Have you made your choice?" cut in Roy coldly.

"I'd do anything you say—go anywhere—give my Bible oath never to come back."

"Perhaps I'd better call Rutherford."

The bad man made a trembling clutch toward him. "Don't you, Mr. Beaudry. I'll—I'll go into the pit," he sobbed.

"Get in, then."

"I know you wouldn't leave me there to starve. That would be an awful thing to do," the killer begged.

"You're finding that out late. It didn't worry you when Dave Dingwell was being starved."

"I hadn't a thing to do with that—not a thing, Mr. Beaudry. Hal Rutherford, he give the order and it was up to me to go through. Honest, that was the way of it."

"And you could starve a girl who needed your help. That was all right, of course."

"Mr. Beaudry, I—I was only learning her a lesson—just kinder playing, y' understand. Why, I've knowed Miss

Beulah ever since she was a little bit of a trick. I wouldn't do her a meanness. It ain't reasonable, now, is it?"

The man fawned on Roy. His hands were shaking with fear. If it would have done any good, he would have fallen on his knees and wept. The sight of him made Roy sick. Was this the way *he* looked when the yellow streak was showing?

"Jump into that pit," he ordered in disgust. "That is, unless you'd rather I would call Rutherford."

Meldrum shambled to the edge, sat down, turned, and slid into the prospect hole.

"I know it's only yore little joke, Mr. Beaudry," he whined. "Mebbe I ain't jest been neighborly with you-all, but what I say is let bygones be bygones. I'm right sorry. I'll go down with you to Battle Butte and tell the boys I done wrong."

"No, you'll stay here."

Beaudry turned away. The muffled scream of the bad man followed him as far as the aspens.

CHAPTER 25

TWO AND A CAMP-FIRE

Roy worked his way through the aspens and returned to the place where he had left Beulah. She was still sleeping soundly and did not stir at his approach. Quietly he built a fire and heated water for coffee. From his saddle-bags he took sandwiches wrapped in a newspaper. Beside the girl he put his canteen, a pocket comb, a piece of soap, and the bandanna he wore around his neck. Then, reluctantly, he awakened her.

"Supper will be served in just five minutes," he announced with a smile.

She glanced at the scant toilet facilities and nodded her head decisively. "Thank you, kind sir. I'll be on hand."

The young woman rose, glanced in the direction of the aspens, gathered up the supplies, and fled to the grove. The eyes of Beaudry followed her flight. The hour of sleep had been enough to restore her resilience. She moved with the strong lightness that always reminded him of wild woodland creatures.

In spite of her promise Beulah was away beyond the time limit. Beaudry became a little uneasy. It was not possible, of course, that Meldrum could have escaped from the pit. And yet—

He called to her. "Is every little thing all right, neighbor?"

"All right," she answered.

A moment later she emerged from the aspens and came toward the camp. She was panting a little, as if she had been running.

"Quite a hill," he commented.

She gave him a quick glance. There was in it shy curiosity, but her dark eyes held, too, an emotion more profound.

"Yes," she said. "It makes one breathe fast."

Miss Rutherford had improved her time. The disorderly locks had been hairpinned into place. From her face all traces of the dried tears were washed. Pit clay no longer stained the riding-skirt.

Sandwiches and coffee made their meal, but neither of

them had ever more enjoyed eating. Beulah was still ravenously hungry, though she restrained her appetite decorously.

"I forgot to tell you that I am lost," he explained. "Unless you can guide me out of this labyrinth of hills, we'll starve to death."

"I can take you straight to the park."

"But we're not going to the park. Everybody is out looking for you. We are to follow Del Oro down to the flats. The trouble is that I've lost Del Oro," he grinned.

"It is just over the hill."

After refreshments he brought up his pinto horse and helped her to the saddle. She achieved the mount very respectably. With a confidential little laugh she took him into the secret of her success.

"I've been practicing with dad. He has to help me up every time I go riding."

They crossed to Del Oro in the dusk and followed the trail by the creek in the moonlight. In the starlight night her dusky beauty set his pulses throbbing. The sweet look of her dark-lashed eyes stirred strange chaos in him. They talked little, for she, too, felt a delicious emotion singing in the currents of her blood. When their shy eyes met, it was with a queer little thrill as if they had kissed each other.

It was late when they reached the flats. There was no sign of Charlton's party.

"The flats run for miles each way. We might wander all night and not find them," Beulah mentioned.

"Then we'll camp right here and look for them in the morning," decided Roy promptly.

Together they built a camp-fire. Roy returned from picketing the horse to find her sitting on a blanket in the dancing light of the flickering flames. Her happy, flushed face was like the promise of a summer day at dawn.

In that immensity of space, with night's million candles far above them and the great hills at their backs, the walls that were between them seemed to vanish.

Their talk was intimate and natural. It had the note of comradeship, took for granted sympathy and understanding.

He showed her the picture of his mother. By the fire glow she studied it intently. Her eyes brimmed with tears.

"She's so lovely and so sweet—and she had to go away and leave her little baby when she was so young. I don't wonder you worship her. I would, too."

Roy did not try to thank her in words. He choked up in his throat and nodded.

"You can see how fine and dainty she was," the girl went on. "I'd rather be like that than anything else in the world—and, of course, I never can be."

"I don't know what you mean," he protested warmly. "You're as fine as they grow."

She smiled, a little wistfully. "Nice of you to say so, but I know better. I'm not a lady. I'm just a harum-scarum, tempery girl that grew up in the hills. If I didn't know it, that wouldn't matter. But I do know it, and so like a little idiot I pity myself because I'm not like nice girls."

"Thank Heaven, you're not!" he cried. "I've never met

a girl fit to hold a candle to you. Why, you're the freest, bravest, sweetest thing that ever lived."

The hot blood burned slowly into her cheek under its dusky coloring. His words were music to her, and yet they did not satisfy.

"You're wrapping it up nicely, but we both know that I'm a vixen when I get angry," she said quietly. "We used to have an old Indian woman work for us. When I was just a wee bit of a thing she called me Little Cactus Tongue."

"That's nothing. The boys were probably always teasing you and you defended yourself. In a way the life you have led has made you hard. But it is just a surface hardness nature has provided as a protection to you."

"Since it is there, I don't see that it helps much to decide why it is a part of me," she returned with a wan little smile.

"But it does," he insisted. "It matters a lot. The point is that it isn't you at all. Some day you'll slough it the way a butterfly does its shell."

"When?" she wanted to know incredulously.

He did not look at her while he blurted out his answer. "When you are happily married to a man you love who loves you."

"Oh! I'm afraid that will be never." She tried to say it lightly, but her face glowed from the heat of an inward fire.

"There's a deep truth in the story of the princess who slept the years away until the prince came along and touched her lips with his. Don't you think lots of people are hampered by their environment? All they need is escape." He suggested this with a shy diffidence.

"Oh, we all make that excuse for ourselves," she answered with a touch of impatient scorn. "I'm all the time doing it. I say if things were different I would be a nice, sweet-tempered, gentle girl and not fly out like that Katharina in Shakespeare's play. But I know all the time it isn't true. We have to conquer ourselves. There is no city of refuge from our own temperaments."

He felt sure there was a way out from her fretted life for this deep-breasted, supple daughter of the hills if she could only find it. She had breathed an atmosphere that made for suspicion and harshness. All her years she had been forced to fight to save herself from shame. But Roy, as he looked at her, imaged another picture of Beulah Rutherford. Little children clung to her knees and called her "Mother." She bent over them tenderly, her face irradiated with love. A man whose features would not come clear strode toward her and the eyes she lifted to his were pools of light.

Beaudry drew a deep breath and looked away from her into the fire. "I wish time would solve my problem as surely as it will yours," he said.

She looked at him eagerly, lips parted, but she would not in words invite his confession.

The young man shaded his eyes with his hand as if to screen them from the fire, but she noticed that the back of his hand hid them from her, too. He found a difficulty in beginning. When at last he spoke, his voice was rough with feeling.

"Of course, you'll despise me—you of all people. How could you help it?"

Her body leaned toward him ever so slightly. Love lit her face like a soft light.

"Shall I? How do you know?"

"It cuts so deep—goes to the bottom of things. If a fellow is wild or even bad, he may redeem himself. But you can't make a man out of a yellow cur. The stuff isn't there." The words came out jerkily as if with some physical difficulty.

"If you mean about coming up to the park, I know about that," she said gently. "Mr. Dingwell told father. I think it was splendid of you."

"No, that isn't it. I knew I was right in coming and that some day you would understand." He dropped the hand from his face and looked straight at her. "Dave didn't tell your father that I had to be flogged into going, did he? He didn't tell him that I tried to dodge out of it with excuses."

"Of course, you weren't anxious to throw up your own affairs and run into danger for a man you had never met. Why should you be wild for the chance? But you went."

"Oh, I went. I had to go. Ryan put it up to me so that there was no escape," was his dogged, almost defiant, answer.

"I know better," the girl corrected quickly. "You put it up to yourself. You're that way."

"Am I?" He flashed a questioning look at her. "Then, since you know that, perhaps you know, too, what—what I'm trying to tell you."

"Perhaps I do," she whispered softly to the fire.

There was panic in his eyes. "—That . . . that I—"

"—That you are sensitive and have a good deal of

imagination," the girl concluded gently.

"No, I'll not feed my vanity with pleasant lies to-night." He gave a little gesture of self-scorn as he rose to throw some dry sticks on the fire. "What I mean and what you mean is that—that I'm an arrant coward." Roy gulped the last words out as if they burned his throat.

"I don't mean that at all," she flamed. "How can you say such a thing about yourself when everybody knows that you're the bravest man in Washington County?"

"No—no. I'm a born trembler." From where he stood beyond the fire he looked across at her with dumb anguish in his eyes. "You say yourself you've noticed it. Probably everybody that knows me has."

"I didn't say that." Her dark eyes challenged his very steadily. "What I said was that you have too much imagination to rush into danger recklessly. You picture it all out vividly beforehand and it worries you. Isn't that the way of it?"

He nodded, ashamed.

"But when the time comes, nobody could be braver than you," she went on. "You've been tried out a dozen times in the last three months. You have always made good."

"Made good! If you only knew!" he answered bitterly.

"Knew what? I saw you down at Hart's when Dan Meldrum ordered you to kneel and beg. But you gamed it out, though you knew he meant to kill you."

He flushed beneath the tan. "I was too paralyzed to move. That's the simple truth."

"Were you too paralyzed to move down at the arcade of the Silver Dollar?" she flashed at him.

"It was the drink in me. I wasn't used to it and it went to my head."

"Had you been drinking that time at the depot?" she asked with a touch of friendly irony.

"That wasn't courage. If it would have saved me, I would have run like a rabbit. But there was no chance. The only hope I had was to throw a fear into him. But all the time I was sick with terror."

She rose and walked round the camp-fire to him. Her eyes were shining with a warm light of admiration. Both hands went out to him impulsively.

"My friend, that is the only kind of courage really worth having. That kind you earn. It is yours because it is born of the spirit. You have fought for it against the weakness of the flesh and the timidity of your own soul. Some men are born without sense or imagination. They don't know enough to be afraid. But the man who tramples down a great fear wins his courage by earning it." She laughed a little, to make light of her own enthusiasm. "Oh, I know I'm preaching like a little prig. But it's the truth, just the same."

At the touch of her fingers his pulses throbbed. But once more he tried to make her understand.

"No, I've had luck all the way through. Do you remember that night at the cabin—before we went up the cañon?"

"Yes."

"Some one shot at me as I ran into the cabin. I was so frightened that I piled all the furniture against the door and hid in the cellar. It was always that way with me. I used to jump if anybody rode up unexpectedly at the ranch. Every little thing set my nerves fluttering."

"But it isn't so now."

"No, not so much."

"That's what I'm telling you," she triumphed. "You came out here from a soft life in town. But you've grown tough because you set your teeth to go through no matter what the cost. I wish I could show you how much I . . . admire you. Dad feels that way, too. So does Ned."

"But I don't deserve it. That's what humiliates me."

"Don't you?" She poured out her passionate protest. "Do you think I don't know what happened back there at the prospect hole? Do you think I don't know that you put Dan Meldrum down in the pit—and him with a gun in his hand? Was it a coward that did that?"

"So you knew that all the time," he cried.

"I heard him calling you—and I went close. Yes, I knew it. But you would never have told me because it might seem like bragging."

"It was easy enough. I wasn't thinking of myself, but of you. He saw I meant business and he wilted."

"You were thinking about me—and you forgot to be afraid," the girl exulted.

"Yes, that was it." A wave of happiness broke over his heart as the sunlight does across a valley at dawn. "I'm always thinking of you. Day and night you fill my thoughts, hillgirl. When I'm riding the range—whatever I do—you're with me all the time."

"Yes."

Her lips were slightly parted, eyes eager and hungry. The heart of the girl drank in his words as the thirsty roots of a rosebush do water. She took a long deep breath and began to tremble.

"I think of you as the daughter of the sun and the wind. Some day you will be the mother of heroes, the wife of a man—"

"Yes," she prompted again, and the face lifted to his was flushed with innocent passion.

The shy invitation of her dark-lashed eyes was not to be denied. He flung away discretion and snatched her into his arms. An inarticulate little sound welled up from her throat, and with a gesture wholly savage and feminine her firm arms crept about his neck and fastened there.

CHAPTER 26

THE SINS OF THE FATHERS

They spoke at first only in that lovers' Esperanto which is made up of fond kisses and low murmurs and soft caresses. From these Beulah was the first to emerge.

"Would you marry a girl off the range?" she whispered. "Would you dare take her home to your people?"

"I haven't any people. There are none of them left but me."

"To your friends, then?"

"My friends will be proud as Punch. They'll wonder how I ever hypnotized you into caring for me."

"But I'm only a hillgirl," she protested. "Are you sure you won't be ashamed of me, dear?"

"Certain sure. I'm a very sensible chap at bottom, and I know when I have the best there is."

"Ah, you think that now because—"

"Because of my golden luck in winning the most wonderful girl I ever met." In the fling of the fire glow he made a discovery and kissed it. "I didn't know before that you had dimples."

"There are lots of things you don't know about me. Some of them you won't like. But if you love me, perhaps you'll forgive them, and then—because I love you—maybe I'll grow out of them. I feel to-night as if anything were possible. The most wonderful thing that ever happened to me has come into my life."

"My heart is saying that, too, sweetheart."

"I love to hear you say that I'm—nice," she confided. "Because, you know, lots of people don't think so. The best people in Battle Butte won't have anything to do with me. I'm one of the Rutherford gang."

The light was full on his face, so that she saw the dawning horror in his eyes.

"What is it? What are you thinking?" she cried.

He gave a little groan and his hands fell slackly from her. "I'd forgotten." The words came in a whisper, as if he spoke to himself rather than to her.

"Forgotten what?" she echoed; and like a flash added: "That I'm a Rutherford. Is that what you mean?"

"That you are the daughter of Hal Rutherford and that I'm the son of John Beaudry."

"You mean that you would be ashamed to marry a Rutherford," she said, her face white in the fire glow.

"No." He brushed her challenge aside and went straight to what was in his mind. "I'm thinking of what happened seventeen years ago," he answered miserably.

"What did happen that could come between you and me to-night?"

"Have you forgotten, too?" He turned to the fire with a deep breath that was half a sob.

"What is it? Tell me," she demanded.

"Your father killed mine at Battle Butte."

A shiver ran through her lithe, straight body. "No . . . No! Say it isn't true, Roy."

"It's true. I was there . . . Didn't they ever tell you about it?"

"I've heard about the fight when Sheriff Beaudry was killed. Jess Tighe had his spine injured in it. But I never knew that dad . . . You're sure of it?" she flung at him.

"Yes. He led the attackers. I suppose he thought of it as a feud. My father had killed one of his people in a gun fight."

She, too, looked into the fire. It was a long time before she spoke, and then in a small, lifeless voice. "I suppose you . . . hate me."

"Hate you!" His voice shook with agitation. "That would make everything easy. But—there is no other woman in the world for me but you."

Almost savagely she turned toward him. "Do you mean that?"

"I never meant anything so much."

"Then what does it matter about our fathers? We have our own lives to live. If we've found happiness we've a right to it. What happened seventeen years ago can't touch us—not unless we let it."

White-lipped, drear-eyed, Roy faced her hopelessly. "I never thought of it before, but it is true what the Bible says about the sins of the fathers. How can I shake hands in friendship with the man who killed mine? Would it be loyal or decent to go into his family and make him my father by marrying his daughter?"

Beulah stood close to him, her eyes burning into his. She was ready to fight for her love to a finish. "Do you think I'm going to give you up now . . . now . . . just when we've found out how much we care . . . because of any reason under heaven outside ourselves? *By God,* no! That's a solemn oath, Roy Beaudry. I'll not let you go."

He did not argue with her. Instead, he began to tell her of his father and his mother. As well as he could remember it he related to her the story of that last ride he had taken with John Beaudry. The girl found herself visioning the pathetic tenderness of the father singing the "li'l'-ole-hawss" song under the stars of their night camp. There flashed to her a picture of him making his stand in the stable against the flood of enemies pouring toward him.

When Roy had finished, she spoke softly. "I'm glad you told me. I know now the kind of man your father was. He loved you more than his own life. He was brave and generous and kind. Do you think he would have nursed a grudge for seventeen years? Do you think he would have asked you to give up your happiness to carry on a feud that ought never to have been?"

"No, but—"

"You are going to marry me, not Hal Rutherford. He is a good man now, however wild he may have been once. But you needn't believe that just because I say so. Wait and see. Be to him just as much or as little as you like.

He'll understand, and so shall I. My people are proud. They won't ask more of you than you care to give. All they'll ask is that you love me—and that's all I ask, dear."

"All you ask now, but later you will be unhappy because there is a gulf between your father and me. You will try to hide it, but I'll know."

"I'll have to take my chance of that," she told him. "I don't suppose that life even with the man you love is all happiness. But it is what I want. It's what I'm not going to let your scruples rob me of."

She spoke with a low-voiced, passionate intensity. The hillgirl was fighting to hold her lover as a creature of the woods does to protect its young. So long as she was sure that he loved her, nothing on earth should come between them. For the moment she was absorbed by the primitive idea that he belonged to her and she to him. All the vital young strength in her rose to repel separation.

Roy, yearning to take into his arms this dusky, brown-cheeked sweetheart of his, became aware that he did not want her to let his arguments persuade her. The fierce, tender egoism of her love filled him with exultant pride.

He snatched her to him and held her tight while his lips found her hot cheeks, her eager eyes, her more than willing mouth.

CHAPTER 27

THE QUICKSANDS

Beulah was too perfect of body, too sound of health, not to revel in such a dawn as swept across the flats next morning. The sun caressed her throat, her bare head, the uplifted face. As the tender light of daybreak was in the hills, so there was a lilt in her heart that found expression in her voice, her buoyant footsteps, and the shine of her eyes. She had slept soundly in Beaudry's blankets while he had lain down in his slicker on the other side of the fire. Already she was quite herself again. The hours of agony in the pit were obliterated. Life was a wholly joyous and beautiful adventure.

She turned back to the camp where Roy was making coffee.

"Am I not to do any of the work?"

At the sound of that deep, sweet voice with its hint of a drawl the young man looked up and smiled. "Not a bit. All you have to do is to drink my coffee and say I'm the best cook you know."

After they had drunk the coffee and finished the sandwiches, Roy saddled.

"They're probably over to the left. Don't you think so?" Beaudry suggested.

"Yes."

There drifted to them the sound of two shots fired in rapid succession.

Roy fired twice in answer. They moved in the direction of the shooting. Again the breeze brought revolver shots.

This time there were three of them.

Beaudry had an odd feeling that this was a call for help from somebody in difficulties. He quickened their pace. The nature of the ground, a good deal of which was deep sand, made fast travel impossible.

"Look!" Beulah pointed forward and to the right.

At the same moment there came a shout. "Help! I'm in the quicksands."

They made out the figure of a man buried to his waist in the dry wash of a creek. A horse stood on the farther bank of the wash. Roy deflected toward the man, Beulah at his heels.

"He must be caught in Dead Man's Sink," the girl explained. "I've never seen it, but I know it is somewhere near here. All my life I've heard of it. Two Norwegians were caught here five years ago. Before help reached them, they were lost."

"Get me a rope—quick," the man in the sand called.

"Why, it's Brad," cried Beulah.

"Yep. Saw the smoke of yore fire and got caught trying to reach you. Can't make it alone. Thought I sure was a goner. You'll have to hurry."

Already Roy was taking the riata from its place below the saddle-horn. From the edge of the wash he made a cast toward the man in the quicksands. The loop fell short.

"You'll have to get into the bed of the stream," suggested Beulah.

Beaudry moved across the sand a few steps and tried again. The distance was still too great.

Already he was beginning to bog down. The soles of

his shoes disappeared in the treacherous sand. When he moved it seemed to him that some monster was sucking at him from below. As he dragged his feet from the sand the sunken tracks filled with mud. He felt the quiver of the river-bed trembling at his weight.

Roy turned to Beulah, the old familiar cold chill traveling up his spine to the roots of his hair. "It won't bear me up. I'm going down," he quavered.

"Let me go, then. I'm lighter," she said eagerly.

She made the proposal in all good faith, with no thought of reflecting on his courage, but it stung her lover like a slap in the face.

"Hurry with that rope!" Charlton sang across. "I'm sinking fast."

"Is there any way for Miss Rutherford to get over to your horse?" asked Roy quickly.

"She can cross the wash two hundred yards below here. It's perfectly safe."

As Roy plunged forward, he gave Beulah orders without turning his head. "You hear, dear. Run down and get across. But go over very carefully. If you come to a bad place, go back at once. When you get over tie Charlton's rope to his saddle-horn and throw him the looped end. The horse will drag him out."

The young woman was off on the run before he had half finished.

Once more Roy coiled and threw the rope. Charlton caught the loop, slipped it over his head, and tightened it under his arms.

"All right. Pull!" he ordered.

Beaudry had no footing to brace himself. Already he

was ankle-deep in the quicksand. It flashed across his mind that he could not fight his own way out without abandoning Charlton. For one panicky moment he was mad to get back to solid ground himself. The next he was tugging with all the strength of his arms at the rope.

"Keep on the job!" encouraged Charlton. "You're pulling my body over a little so that the weight is on new sand. If Beulah gets here in time, I'll make it."

Roy pulled till his muscles ached. His own feet were sliding slowly from under him. The water-bubbles that oozed out of the sand were now almost at his high boot-tops. It was too late to think of retreat. He must go through whether he wanted to or not.

He cast one look down the dry river-bed. Beulah was just picking her way across. She might get over in time to save Charlton, but before they made it back across to him, he would be lost.

He wanted to scream aloud to her his urgent need, to beg her, for Heaven's sake, to hurry. The futility of it he knew. She was already running with the knowledge to wing her feet that a man's life hung in the balance. Besides, Charlton was not shrieking his fears out. He was calling cheerful words of hope across the quaking morass of sand that separated them. There was no use in making a gibbering idiot of one's self. Beaudry clenched his jaws tight on the cries that rose like a thermometer of terror in his throat.

With every ounce of strength that was in him he fought, meanwhile, for the life of the man at the other end of the rope. Before Beulah reached Charlton, Roy was in deeper than his knees. He shut his eyes and pulled like a machine. It seemed an eternity before Charlton called to him to let go the rope.

A new phase of his danger seared like a flame across the brain of Beaudry. He had dragged himself from a perpendicular position. As soon as he let loose of the rope he would begin to sink forward. This would reduce materially the time before his face would sink into the sand.

Why not hang on and let the horse drag him out, too? He had as much right to live as Charlton. Was there any law of justice that forced him to throw away the rope that was his only hope?

But he knew the tough little cowpony could not drag two heavy men from the quicksands at the same time. If he held tight, Charlton, too, would be sacrificed. His fingers opened.

Roy watched the struggle on the opposite side of the wash. Charlton was in almost to his arm-pits. The horse braced its feet and pulled. Beulah, astride the saddle, urged it to the task again and again. At first by imperceptible gains, then inch by inch, the man was dragged from the mire that fought with a thousand clinging tentacles for its prey.

Not till Charlton was safe on the bank did Beulah realize the peril of Beaudry. One glance across the river showed her that he was sliding face downward to a shifting grave. With an anguished little cry she released the rope from Charlton's body, flung herself to the saddle again, and dashed down the bank of the creek.

Roy lost count of time. His face was sliding down toward the sand. Soon his mouth and nostrils would be stopped. He believed that it was a question of minutes with him.

Came the swift pounding of hoofs and Beulah's clear, ringing voice.

"Hold your hands straight out, Roy."

His back was toward. her, so that he did not see what she meant to do. But he obeyed blindly. With a wrench first one hand and then the other came free from the sand and wavered into the air heavily. A rope sang, dropped over his arms and head, tightened with a jerk around his waist.

Two monsters seemed to be trying to tear him in two. A savage wrench of pain went through him jaggedly. At short intervals this was repeated.

In spite of the suction of the muddy sand he felt its clutch giving way. It loosened a little here, a little there. His body began to move. After a long tug he came out at last with a rush. But he left his high cowpuncher's boots behind. They remained buried out of sight in the sand. He had literally been dragged out of them.

Roy felt himself pulled shoreward. From across the quicksands came Charlton's whoop of triumph. Presently Beulah was stooping over him with tender little cries of woe and joy.

He looked at her with a wan, tired smile. "I didn't think you'd make it in time." In a moment he added: "I was horribly afraid. God, it was awful!"

"Of course. Who wouldn't have been?" She dismissed his confession as of no importance. "But it's all over now. I want to hug you tight to make sure you're here, boy."

"There's no law against it," he said with feeble humor.

"No, but—" With a queer little laugh she glanced across the river toward her former lover. "I don't think I had better."

Charlton joined them a few minutes later. He went straight to Roy and offered his hand.

"The feud stuff is off, Mr. Beaudry. Beulah will tell you that I started in to make you trouble. Well, there's nothing doing in that line. I can't fight the man who saved my life at the risk of his own."

"Oh, well!" Roy blushed. "I just threw you a rope."

"You bogged down some," Charlton returned dryly. "I've known men who would have thought several times before throwing that rope from where you did. They would have hated to lose their boots."

Beulah's eyes shone. "Oh, Brad, I'm so glad. I do want you two to be friends."

"Do you?" As he looked at her, the eyes of the young hillman softened. He guessed pretty accurately the state of her feelings. Beaudry had won and he had lost. Well, he was going to be a good loser this time. "What you want goes with me this time, Boots. The way you yanked me out of the sinks was painful, but thorough. I'll be a friend to Mr. Beaudry if he is of the same opinion as you. And I'll dance at his wedding when it comes off."

She cried out at that, but Charlton noticed that she made no denial. Neither did Roy. He confined his remarks to the previous question, and said that he would be very glad of Charlton's friendship.

"Good enough. Then I reckon we better light out for

camp with the glad news that Beulah has been found. You can tell me all about it on the way," the hillman suggested.

Beulah dropped from her horse ten minutes later into the arms of Ned Rutherford. Quite unexpectedly to himself, that young man found himself filled with emotion. He caught his sister in his arms and held her as if he never intended to let the sobbing girl go. His own voice was not at all steady.

"Boots—Boots . . . Honey-bug . . . Where you-all been?" he asked, choking up suddenly.

CHAPTER 28

PAT RYAN EVENS AN OLD SCORE

Dingwell, the coffee-pot in one hand and a tin cup in the other, hailed his partner cheerfully. "Come over here, son, and tell me who you traded yore boots to."

"You and Brad been taking a mud bath, Mr. Beaudry?" asked one of the Lazy Double D riders.

Roy told them, with reservations, the story of the past twenty-four hours. Dave listened, an indifferent manner covering a quick interest. His young friend had done for himself a good stroke of business. There could no longer be any question of the attitude of the Rutherfords toward him, since he had been of so great service to Beulah. Charlton had renounced his enmity, the ground cut from beneath his feet. Word had reached camp only an hour before of the death of Tighe. This left of Beaudry's foes only Hart, who did not really count, and Dan Meldrum, at the present moment facing starvation in a prospect hole. On the whole, it had been a surprisingly good twenty-four hours for Roy. His partner saw this, though he did not know the best thing Roy had won out of it.

"Listens fine," the old-timer commented when the young man had finished.

"Can you rustle me a pair of boots from one of the boys, Dave? Size number eight. I've got to run back up Del Oro to-day."

"Better let me go, son," Dave proposed casually.

"No. It's my job to turn the fellow loose."

"Well, see he doesn't get the drop on you. I wouldn't trust him far as I could throw a bull by the tail."

Dingwell departed to borrow the boots and young Rutherford came over to Beaudry. Out of the corner of his eye Roy observed that Beulah was talking with the little Irish puncher, Pat Ryan.

Rutherford plunged awkwardly into his thanks. His sister had made only a partial confidant of him, but he knew that she was under obligations to Beaudry for the rescue from Meldrum. The girl had not dared tell her brother that the outlaw was still within his reach. She knew how impulsively his anger would move to swift action.

"We Rutherfords ain't liable to forget this, Mr. Beaudry. Dad has been 'most crazy since Boots disappeared. He'll sure want to thank you himself soon as he gets a chance," blurted Ned.

"I happened to be the lucky one to find her; that's all," Roy deprecated.

"Sure. I understand. But you did find her. That's the

point. Dad won't rest easy till he's seen you. I'm going to take sis right home with me. Can't you come along?"

Roy wished he could, but it happened that he had other fish to fry. He shook his head reluctantly.

Dingwell returned with a pair of high-heeled cow-puncher's boots. "Try these on, son. They belong to Dusty. The lazy hobo wasn't up yet. If they fit you, he'll ride back to the ranch in his socks."

After stamping about in the boots to test them, Roy decided, that they would do. "They fit like a coat of paint," he said.

"Say, son, I'm going to hit the trail with you on that little jaunt you mentioned," his partner announced definitely.

Roy was glad. He had of late been fed to repletion with adventure. He did not want any more, and with Dingwell along he was not likely to meet it. Already he had observed that adventures generally do not come to the adventurous, but to the ignorant and the incompetent. Dave moved with a smiling confidence along rough trails that would have worried his inexperienced partner. To the old-timer these difficulties were not dangers at all, because he knew how to meet them easily.

They rode up Del Oro by the same route Roy and Beulah had followed the previous night. Before noon they were close to the prospect hole where Roy had left the rustler. The sound of voices brought them up in their tracks.

They listened. A whine was in one voice; in the other was crisp command.

"Looks like some one done beat us to it," drawled

Dingwell. "We'll move on and see what's doing."

They topped the brow of a hill.

A bow-legged little man with his back to them was facing Dan Meldrum.

"I'm going along with yez as far as the border. You'll keep moving lively till ye hit the hacienda of old Porf. Diaz. And you'll stay there. Mind that now, Dan. Don't—"

The ex-convict broke in with the howl of a trapped wolf. "You've lied to me. You brought yore friends to kill me."

The six-gun of the bad man blazed once—twice. In answer the revolver of the bandy-legged puncher barked out, fired from the hip. Meldrum staggered, stumbled, pitched forward into the pit. The man who had killed him walked slowly forward to the edge and looked down. He stood poised for another shot if one should prove necessary.

Dave joined him.

"He's dead as a stuck shote, Pat," the cattleman said gravely.

Ryan nodded. "You saw he fired first, Dave."

"Yes." After a moment he added: "You've saved the hangman a job, Pat. I don't know anybody Washington County could spare better. There'll be no complaint, I reckon."

The little Irishman shook his head. "That would go fine if you had shot him, Dave, or if Mr. Beaudry here had. But with me it's different. I've been sivinteen years living down a reputation as a hellion. This ain't going to do me any good. Folks will say it was a case of one bad man wiping out another. They'll say I've gone back to being a gunman. I'll be in bad sure as taxes."

Dingwell looked at him, an idea dawning in his mind. Why not keep from the public the name of the man who had shot Meldrum? The position of the wound and the revolver clenched in the dead man's hand would show he had come to his end in fair fight. The three of them might sign a statement to the effect that one of them had killed the fellow in open battle. The doubt as to which one would stimulate general interest. No doubt the gossips would settle on Beaudry as the one who had done it. This would still further enhance his reputation as a good man with whom not to pick trouble.

"Suits me if it does Roy," the cattleman said, speaking his thoughts aloud. "How about it, son? Pat is right. This will hurt him, but it wouldn't hurt you or me a bit. Say the word and all three of us will refuse to tell which one shot Meldrum."

"I'm willing," Roy agreed. "And I've been looking up ancient history, Mr. Ryan. I don't think you were as bad as you painted yourself to me once. I'm ready to shake hands with you whenever you like."

The little Irishman flushed. He shook hands with shining eyes.

"That's why I was tickled when Miss Beulah asked me to come up and turn loose that coyote. It's a God's truth that I hoped he'd fight. I wanted to do you a good bit of wolf-killing if I could. And I've done it . . . and I'm not sorry. He had it coming if iver a man had."

"Did you say that Beulah Rutherford sent you up here?" asked Roy.

"She asked me to come. Yis."

"Why?"

"I can only guess her reasons. She didn't want you to come and she couldn't ask Ned for fear he would gun the fellow. So she just picked on a red-headed runt of an Irishman."

"While we're so close, let's ride across to Huerfano Park," suggested Dave. "I haven't been there in twenty years."

That suited Roy exactly. As they rode across the hills his mind was full of Beulah. She had sent Ryan up so that he could get Meldrum away before her lover arrived. Was it because she was afraid Roy might show the white feather? Or was it because she feared for his safety? He wished he knew.

CHAPTER 29

A NEW LEAF

Hal Rutherford himself met the three riders as they drew up at the horse ranch. He asked no verbal questions, but his eyes ranged curiously from one to another.

" 'Light, gentlemen. I been wanting to see you especially, Mr. Beaudry," he said.

"I reckon you know where we've been, Hal," answered Dave after he had dismounted.

"I reckon."

"We got a little news for public circulation. You can pass the word among the boys. Dan Meldrum was shot three hours ago beside the pit where Miss Beulah was imprisoned. His body is in the prospect hole now. You might send some lads with spades to bury him."

"One of you shot him."

"You done guessed it, Hal. One of us helped him out of that pit intending to see he hit the dust to Mexico. Dan was loaded to the guards with suspicions. He chose to make it a gunplay. Fired twice. The one of us that took him out of the pit fired back and dropped him first crack. All of us saw the affair. It happened just as I've told you."

"But which of you—?"

"That's the only point we can't remember. It was one of us, but we've forgotten which one."

"Suits me if it does you. I'll thank all three of you, then." Rutherford cleared his throat and plunged on. "Boys, to-day kinder makes an epoch in Huerfano Park. Jess Tighe died yesterday and Dan Meldrum to-day. They were both bad citizens. There were others of us that were bad citizens, too. Well, it's rightabout face for us. We travel broad trails from now on. Right now the park starts in to make a new record for itself."

Dave offered his hand, and with it went the warm smile that made him the most popular man in Washington County. "Listens fine, Hal. I sure am glad to hear you say so."

"I niver had any kick against the Rutherfords. They were open and aboveboard, anyhow, in all their diviltry," contributed Ryan to the pact of peace.

Nobody looked at Roy, but he felt the weight of their thoughts. All four of them bore in mind the death of John

Beaudry. His son spoke quietly.

"Mr. Rutherford, I've been thinking of my father a good deal these last few days. I want to do as he would have me do about this thing. I'm not going to chop my words. He gave his life to bring law and order into this country. The men who killed him were guilty of murder. That's an ugly word, but it's the true one."

The grim face of the big hillman did not twitch. "I'll take the word from you. Go on."

"But I've been thinking more and more that he would want me to forget that. Tighe and Meldrum are gone. Sheriff Beaudry worked for the good of the community. That is all he asked. It is for the best interest of Washington County that we bury the past. If you say so, I'll shake hands on that and we'll all face to the future, just as you say."

Dingwell grinned. "Hooray! Big Chief Dave will now make oration. You've got the right idea, son. I knew Jack Beaudry. There wasn't an atom of revenge in his game body. His advice would have been to shake hands. That's mine, too."

The hillman and Roy followed it.

Upon the porch a young woman appeared. "I've written those letters for you, dad," she called.

Roy deserted the peace conference at once and joined her.

"Oh! I didn't know it was you," she cried. "I'm so glad you came this way. Was it . . . all right?"

"Right as the wheat. Why did you send Pat up Del Oro?"

She looked at him with eyes incredibly kind and shy.

"Because I . . . didn't want to run any chance of losing my new beau."

"Are you sure that was your only reason?"

"Certain sure. I didn't trust Meldrum, and . . . I thought you had taken chances enough with him. So I gave Mr. Ryan an opportunity."

"He took it," her lover answered gravely.

She glanced at him quickly. "You mean—?"

"Never mind what I mean now. We've more important things to talk about. I haven't seen you for eight hours, and thirty-three minutes."

Rutherford turned his guests over to Ned, who led the way to the stable. The ranchman joined the lovers. He put an arm around Beulah.

"Boots has done told me about you two, Mr. Beaudry. I'm eternally grateful to you for bringing back my little girl to me, and if you-all feel right sure you care for each other I've got nothing to say but 'God bless you.' You're a white man. You're decent. I believe you'll be kind to her."

"I'm going to try to the best I know, Mr. Rutherford."

"You'd better, young man." The big rancher swallowed a lump in his throat and passed to another phase of the subject. "Boots was telling me about how it kinder stuck in yore craw to marry the daughter of Hal Rutherford, seeing as how things happened the way they did. Well, I'm going to relieve yore mind. She's the one that has got the forgiving to do, not you. She knew it all the time, too, but she didn't tell it. Beulah is the daughter of my brother Anse. I took her from the arms of her dying mother when she was a little trick that couldn't crawl.

She's not the daughter of the man that shot yore father. She's the daughter of the man yore father shot."

"Oh!" gasped Roy.

Beulah went to her lover arrow-swift.

"My dear . . . my dear! What does it matter now? Dad says my father was killed in fair fight. He had set himself against the law. It took his life. Your father didn't."

"But—"

"Oh, his was the hand. But he was sheriff. He did only his duty. That's true, isn't it, dad?"

"I reckon."

Her strong young hands gripped tightly those of her lover. She looked proudly into his eyes with that little flare of feminine ferocity in hers.

"I won't have it any other way, Roy Beaudry. You're the man I'm going to marry, the man who is going to be the father of my children if God gives me any. No blood stands between us—nothing but the memory of brave men who misunderstood each other and were hurt because of it. Our marriage puts an end forever to even the memory of the wrong they did each other. That is the way it is to me—and that's the way it has got to be to you, too."

Roy laughed softly, tears in his eyes. As he looked at her eager young beauty the hot life in his pulses throbbed. He snatched her to him with an ardor as savage as her own.

Center Point Publishing
600 Brooks Road • PO Box 1
Thorndike ME 04986-0001 USA

(207) 568-3717

US & Canada:
1 800 929-9108